P9-CBD-231

SPY
PENGUINS

SAM HAY

Illustrated by MAREK JAGUCKI

SQUARE
FISH

FEIWEL AND FRIENDS · NEW YORK

SQUARE FISH

An imprint of Macmillan Publishing Group, LLC
120 Broadway, New York, NY 10271
mackids.com

Square Fish and the Square Fish logo are trademarks of Macmillan and are
used by Feiwel and Friends under license from Macmillan.

Our books may be purchased in bulk for promotional, educational, or business
use. Please contact your local bookseller or the Macmillan Corporate and
Premium Sales Department at (800) 221-7945 ext. 5442 or by email
at MacmillanSpecialMarkets@macmillan.com.

Library of Congress Cataloging-in-Publication Data is available.
ISBN 978-1-250-21104-0 (paperback) / ISBN 978-1-250-18839-7 (ebook)

Originally published in the United States by Feiwel and Friends
First Square Fish edition, 2019
Book designed by Carol Ly
Square Fish logo designed by Filomena Tuosto

3 5 7 9 10 8 6 4 2

AR: 4.5 / LEXILE: 650L

FOR ALICE AND ARCHIE
AND PENGUIN AFICIONADOS
EVERYWHERE

SPY PENGUINS

Secret Agent 00Zero (also known as Jackson to his mom) wiped the frost off his icePad and handed it to his best friend, Quigley. "Ready?"

"Sure!" Quigley said, pointing the icePad camera at the sled behind Jackson. "The Ice Blaster looks awesome on-screen."

Jackson smiled. "Great, but remember to get *me* in the shot, too."

Quigley's face turned shrimp pink. "Oh, yeah," he mumbled, stepping back to include Jackson in the picture. "Sorry."

Jackson sighed. Quigley was supposed to be filming Jackson riding the sled down Frostbite Ridge—the giant iceberg above Rookeryville, where they lived. But so far it looked like the video was going to be ALL sled and NO Jackson. *But,* Jackson reminded himself, *this is no ordinary sled.* It was Quigley's latest and greatest invention: a super-speedy, ice-blasting spy-getaway vehicle with four giant rocket blasters on the back. A sled so epic, Jackson thought it could be the answer to his dreams . . .

"Let's do this!" Jackson put on his sunglasses and shook out his feathers so they stood up on end, making him look tough. Because you had to be tough if you wanted to be a secret agent working for the FBI (the Frosty Bureau of Investigation). And joining the FBI was the reason they were shooting the video. It was the thing Jackson wanted more than anything else in the world. Even more than he wanted his favorite flipper-ball team, the Toothfish, to win the league pennant. All he had to do was convince the FBI that they needed him.

Quigley pointed the icePad at Jackson. "FBI audition video, take one."

Jackson took a deep breath. "Hi, I'm Secret Agent 00Zero," he said, staring into the camera with a serious look on his face. "I'm here today to show you—the bosses at the FBI—why you should hire me as a trainee secret agent. Oh, and you'll definitely want to hire my buddy, too—"

Quigley spun the icePad around to himself. "Hi there!" He beamed into the lens before turning it back to Jackson.

"That was Secret Agent Q," Jackson said. "We've been friends since we were eggs. He's the greatest gadget inventor in Rookeryville—"

Quigley coughed.

"Err, make that the WORLD!" Jackson winked at Quigley, then went back to looking serious again. "This is one of Agent Q's inventions." He waggled his flipper at the sled. "And

I'm going to use it to demonstrate my secret-agent driving skills. Let's do this!" Jackson gave a flippers-up, then climbed aboard the sled. He gripped the steering wheel with both wings and pushed his foot down on the accelerator pedal.

Nothing happened.

"Err—Quigley," Jackson whispered. "I'm still here."

Quigley peered around the side of the ice-Pad. "Maybe it just needs a shove."

As Quigley's foot made contact with the back of the sled there was a loud *VAROOM!* The rocket blasters exploded to life, burping out a plume of stinky seaweed-smelling smoke and shooting the sled forward, nearly knocking Jackson off his seat.

"Whoa!" he breathed as he zoomed down the slope, his spiky yellow crest flapping in the icy wind. *If this doesn't show them, nothing will!*

VHOOSH! He steered the sled left to avoid a giant boulder.

VHOOSH! He steered right to miss three dad penguins out for a huddle with their eggs.

VHOOSH! He steered left to avoid heading down the path to the Cliff of Doom, but suddenly the sled seemed to hiccup. And then splutter. And then—

"*Ahhhhhh!*" Jackson screamed. Or he would have if he hadn't been a secret agent, because secret agents weren't allowed to scream, even when they were racing down an iceberg and the steering wheel of their getaway vehicle had just come off in their flippers.

"Help!" Jackson yelled, breaking the secret-agent rule of never shouting for help on a secret spy mission, on account of the sled having, by itself, turned right—a VERY, VERY, EXTREMELY HARD RIGHT—which meant it was now out of control and hurtling toward the Cliff of Doom.

Don't panic, Jackson told himself. *Secret agents never panic.* Jackson knew this because his Uncle Bryn was a real-life secret agent with the FBI. And Uncle Bryn never panicked, even when he mislaid his secret-agent tool kit, which happened at least twice a week.

Jackson looked desperately at the dashboard. *There has to be a way to stop this thing. . . . Wait. . . . What's that?* He noticed a small red button with Quigley's squiggly writing underneath. Jackson tried to read the writing, hoping it might say p-a-r-a-c-h-u-t-e. But instead, "M-R-jen-C," he read aloud. *Huh?*

There was no time to figure it out. He hit the button and held his breath as the ground below him vanished and he shot over the Cliff of Doom.

For one feather-clenching moment nothing happened. The sled just sort of sailed through the sky, minding its own business. And Jackson felt a bubble of hope in his belly. *Maybe this is actually a flying secret spy-getaway vehicle,* he thought. *Maybe Quigley really is a genius—*

Or maybe not. Jackson gripped the sides of the sled as it suddenly stopped minding its own business and began f-a-l-l-i-n-g. . . .

"HELP!" Jackson tried slapping the M-R-jen-C button again and again. But nothing happened. "Sucking squids! Do something!" he yelled at the sled.

And it did.

A giant split appeared in the floor between Jackson's feet.

"Noooo! I'm doomed," he groaned.

But just then there was a loud *whoosh* and four enormous shapes burst out of the split. And the sled suddenly yo-yoed back up into the air, jerking and twisting as four giant inflating helium balloons bobbed against one another.

"Quigley, you *are* a genius!" Jackson breathed as he gently glided up, up, up through the air over Rookeryville.

Jackson craned his neck over the side. He could see his school . . . and the park . . . and Brain Freezers. Brain Freezers was the best milk shake shack in Rookeryville; it had amazing seaweed shakes. Jackson tried to see if anyone was sitting in his and Quigley's favorite seats in the window. Mission Control, they called it. It was the place where they hatched all their best FBI-joining schemes.

Jackson was so busy thinking about Brain Freezers that he didn't spot the large shape looming out of the clouds toward him until it was too late.

"Stop! No!" He shook his flippers wildly at the gigantic bird soaring straight toward him. "LOOK OUT!" he yelled.

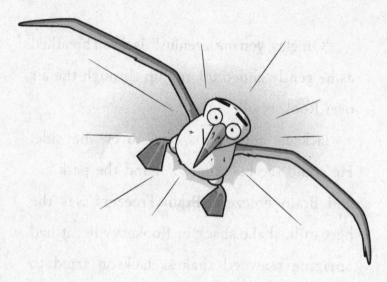

But the albatross obviously didn't speak penguin.

SQUAWK! And suddenly the sky was a messy jumble of wings, sled, feathers, beaks, balloons, claws—SUPER-SHARP BALLOON-POPPING CLAWS—

And—

POP! POP! POP! POP! H-i-s-sssssssss.

For the second time in five minutes Jackson found himself dropping from the sky. He shut his eyes as the air whistled past his ears and he waited for the *splat*.

Except it wasn't a *SPLAT*. It was more of a *sploosh*, as everything turned greeny-blue and bubbly and wet, and slightly fish-pooey stinky.

"The sea!" Jackson shouted, sending a stream of air bubbles out of his beak. "I landed in the sea." Which was odd, because he was pretty sure he'd been right above the town when he'd started falling. *But I've always been a lucky kind of penguin,* he reminded himself as he swam upward, scattering a group of strange-looking giant fish. *Must remember to tell the FBI how lucky I am. All secret agents need a feather or two of luck.*

Jackson was still thinking about how lucky he was when he reached the surface and poked his head out—

"Huh?" He looked around. This did NOT look like the sea. It was more like . . . a pond, he guessed, glancing around. *A large pond with*

buildings all around and—and— Wait! Who
are all those scary-looking penguin dudes in
dark glasses with ICE LASERS POINTING
AT MY HEAD?

"FREEZE!" one shouted. "Or we'll ice you
into oblivion."

"**S**top! Don't shoot!" Jackson held up his flippers, his heart racing.

One of the penguins took off his sunglasses. "Jackson? Is that you?"

Jackson took off his sunglasses, too, and blinked at the familiar face. "Uncle Bryn?" Relief flooded through his feathers. The other penguins lowered their ice lasers, but they were still staring at him. And then a tiny bell sounded in the back of Jackson's brain and his beak fell open in surprise. "Oh!" he breathed. "Is this an FBI stakeout?"

As soon as he said it he wished he hadn't, because secret agents weren't allowed to talk about their work. NOT EVER! (Though Jackson's Uncle Bryn wasn't actually good at this rule. Just the week before he'd come over for a sea-lettuce stir-fry and blabbed something about having to leave soon because they were planning an FBI operation to take down a super-baddie called Bad Beak.)

"I won't tell," Jackson said, looking around at all the agents. "You can trust me." The penguins began shuffling their feet and clearing their throats, sliding their ice lasers back into their suits.

"Sorry, guys," Uncle Bryn mumbled to his colleagues. "Can you give us a minute? Here, Jackson, grab my flipper."

"What's this all about?" Jackson asked, climbing out of the water and shaking his feathers dry.

"I can't talk about my work, Jackson, you know that," Uncle Bryn said loudly, so his colleagues could hear.

"What is this place, anyway?" Jackson peered at the large notice boards with pictures of fish on them around the pond, and a giant sign saying:

STRICTLY **NO** SWIMMING AND **NO** EATING THE EXHIBITS!
THESE FISH ARE PROTECTED UNDER ROOKERYVILLE LAW

"The City Aquarium," Uncle Bryn whispered. "Where they keep the rare fish."

Jackson looked back at the pool he'd just climbed out of. So that was why the fish he'd swum past had looked so strange. "Oh, yeah," he said, nodding. "I remember now. We came here for a school trip in first grade. Hoff Rockface ate a super-rare shrimp and Mrs. Cockle-Hopper made him barf it back up. She told Hoff if he didn't, he'd be locked up in jail." Jackson glanced around. "The shrimp was fine, by the way. It's probably still here somewhere."

Uncle Bryn nodded. But he was watching his colleagues, who were in a huddle now, whispering to one another. "I think maybe you'd better go home now, Jackson," he said quietly. "My boss isn't the friendliest penguin in Rookeryville."

As if she'd heard him, a large emperor penguin with a very long beak broke away from the huddle and waved her flipper. "That's it, guys. The operation is canceled. The target is not going to show now. Not after all this fuss." She turned her glare on Jackson. "Stupid hatchling!" she hissed.

Jackson felt his cheeks burning. *Hatchling?* He wished the ground would swallow him up, blue whale–style.

Uncle Bryn shuffled his feet in embarrassment.

"I'm so sorry," Jackson said quietly.

"It's okay," Uncle Bryn said. "Not your fault."

"Return to base!" the boss penguin shouted. "Except for you." She waddled over and poked Uncle Bryn in the chest with a sharp flipper. "Did you tell that hatchling about our mission?" She glanced at Jackson. "Well? Did you?"

"N-n-no, boss," Uncle Bryn spluttered.

She narrowed her eyes. "I've seen him before. I never forget a beak."

Jackson gulped and quickly hid his beak behind his flipper. But it was true. A few weeks before, when Uncle Bryn had come by for a barbecue and accidentally left his spy camera behind, Jackson had taken it to him at the FBI's secret base. It actually wasn't a very secret base, on account of Uncle Bryn having put a sticker on his spy camera that said, PROPERTY OF SECRET AGENT BRYN ROCKFLOPPER. IF FOUND, PLEASE RETURN TO FBI HEADQUARTERS, THE SECRET BASE, 1 HIDDEN HARBOR DRIVE, ROOKERYVILLE.

P.S. PLEASE DON'T TELL ANYONE. Jackson had bumped into Uncle Bryn's boss at the door, and she hadn't been very welcoming. Nope. Not one bit. More like an angry walrus with a bad toothache.

"I've warned you before, Agent Rockflopper," the boss penguin hissed at Uncle Bryn. "If you mess up again, you'll be out of the FBI and back on traffic duty before you can fluff your tail feathers!" She shook her head. "Consider yourself officially on notice. One more mistake and you'll be out—FOREVER!" She turned and waddled off, with the other agents following behind.

Uncle Bryn sighed. "Bye, Jackson." He patted his nephew on the head. "I'll see you soon. Oh, look—" As Uncle Bryn walked past the pond, he reached down and pulled out the sled, which had resurfaced. Water *skoosh*ed out the sides. "Maybe I can help you fix it up sometime." Uncle Bryn handed it to Jackson. "It looks like I might have a lot of free time soon." He followed his colleagues into the main building of the aquarium, hunched over, his beak turned down.

A wave of worry passed through Jackson's feathers. He shivered. Was Uncle Bryn about to lose his job on account of him? If only he hadn't crash-landed right in the middle of the FBI stakeout. *Maybe I should go tell Uncle Bryn's boss how awesome he is,* Jackson thought. But would Uncle Bryn's boss listen to him? Jackson doubted it. And anyway, he wasn't sure he was brave enough to face her again. She was one scary penguin.

Jackson glanced around the fish pond. If he knew what the FBI had been doing here, then maybe he could help Uncle Bryn with his mission. *That's it! I'll crack this case for him. No way will Uncle Bryn lose his job then.* Jackson straightened up. He put his dark glasses back on. "Let's do this!" he said out loud.

But there was one tiny, krill-size problem with this plan. Jackson didn't have the slightest clue what the mission was about.

"**Jackson! Jackson!**" **A door burst open** and Quigley came rushing out. "Did you just see a whole gang of serious-looking penguin dudes with dark glasses? I passed them in the hall. They looked a lot like—"

"The FBI?" Jackson nodded. "Yeah, they were here, just now."

"Awesome!" Quigley beamed. "Did they see the sled? If not, I got it all on video." He waggled the icePad at Jackson.

"Even the part when you crashed into the albatross. The FBI will love that. It shows you can think on your flippers. But, hey, remind me to add albatross bumpers to the sled for next time."

"Next time—uh?" Jackson raised his eyebrows.

"But the emergency balloons were neat, weren't they?" Quigley puffed up his feathers and grinned. "I saw them inflate with my new bin-ice-ulars." He wafted a pair of frosty-looking eyeglasses at Jackson. "Hard ice crystals make THE best magnification lenses. Want to try them?"

But Jackson was staring at something else—something small and black that was floating in the pond. He reached down into the water. "Uncle Bryn's radio transmitter! He must have dropped it when he got the sled out for me."

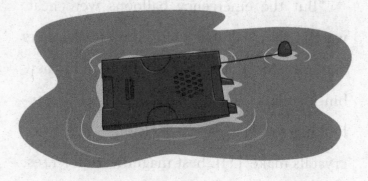

Quigley's eyes lit up. "Oooh, a real FBI radio. I'd love to open it up and see what's—"

"Stop!" Jackson moved it out of Quigley's reach. "You can't take it apart. Uncle Bryn needs it. He's already in trouble. If his boss finds out he lost it . . ." Jackson shuddered. "Remember the trouble he got into when he lost his fit-any-lock skeleton keys at our house playing flipper ball?"

Quigley nodded. "But you've got to admit they were useful. Those sour squid chews we found in your sister's secret box were awesome."

Jackson grinned. He'd enjoyed snooping around in the bedroom of his grumpy big sister, Finola, and using the spy keys to unlock her secret strongbox and raid her candy stash. Especially when he'd also found his missing flipper-ball trading card inside, the ultra-rare one of super striker Rod Ripped-Hopper that he'd lost ages before. What it was doing inside Finola's strongbox, Jackson had no idea. And even though Finola had exploded when she found out and Jackson's mom had punished him by making him bathe the egg (his soon-to-be sibling) for three days in a row, it had all been worth it to get his flipper-ball card back.

"What was the FBI doing here, anyway?" Quigley asked.

Jackson leaned in closer. "They were on a mission," he whispered. "But Uncle Bryn couldn't tell me what it was about. If we could find out, we could maybe crack the case for them. That would definitely help Uncle Bryn. AND they might let us join. . . . Hey," Jackson said, peering across the pond. "Isn't that Lily from school? Yes, it is. HI, LILY!" Jackson waved to a small chinstrap penguin carrying a tray of white tubs and coming through a door marked PRIVATE.

"Oh, hi, Jackson. Hi, Quigley." Lily waddled over. "Are you here for the koi carp feeding time?" She held out a tub of small brown balls.

"Um, yeah," Jackson said. "Thanks. Do you work here?"

"I help my dad on Saturdays. He's a keeper here." Lily sniffled. "But he might not be for much longer." She shuffled her little webbed feet and looked away. "They're blaming him, see."

"For what?" Jackson tried not to look too excited, but his adventure detector had started to sound. He was pretty sure whatever was troubling Lily had something to do with why Uncle Bryn and the FBI had been there.

"I'm not supposed to say," Lily whispered.

"We won't tell," Jackson said, moving closer.

Quigley nodded and pretended to zip his beak.

"Okay," Lily said. "Don't say anything, but someone's stealing the rare fish from the aquarium."

"So *that's* why the FBI was here!" Jackson nodded to Quigley. "It *was* a stakeout. I knew it."

Lily's eyes flashed and her beak went up. "The police think Dad's involved."

"Why?" Jackson frowned. "If your dad is a keeper here, why would he want to steal his own fish?"

"Because he knows how valuable they are," Lily said. "They think he's selling them off to a private rare-fish collector. Look—watch this. . . ." Lily tipped one of the tubs of fish food into the pool. For a few seconds nothing happened, but then shadows began to form. Fish-shaped shadows.

"They're enormous!" Jackson gasped as the fish surfaced to feed.

"And so sparkly," Quigley added, peering over his glasses. "I wonder how they achieve that iridescent effect. It's probably got something to do with constructive light interference—two waves of light working together."

"All I know is that these fish are extremely rare," Lily said. "And very valuable. They're giant blue Antarctic koi carp. And we've lost six since Sunday."

"Don't you have a burglar alarm?" Quigley asked, pushing his glasses up his nose. "I could make one for you. I've got one on my bedroom door. If anyone comes in—"

"They get splattered in seagull poop," Jackson finished for him, and grinned. "Your mom told my mom that she got gunged."

Quigley shrugged. "She should have knocked before she came in."

"Of course we've got an alarm. And cameras," Lily said. "But whoever is stealing the fish still gets in."

Jackson looked around the aquarium. *If the thieves aren't breaking in, then how are they stealing the fish?* He glanced up at the sky. "Wait a minute—maybe the thieves are flying in, like I did?"

But Lily wasn't listening. "Seventeen, eighteen, nineteen," she counted, peering into the fish pool. "Oh, no!" She gasped. "Another one's gone. We had twenty fish half an hour ago."

Jackson crouched down next to the pond. "Maybe one of them is hiding at the bottom," he suggested. "I could dive in and take a look."

"No, it's okay." Lily sighed. "They never miss feeding time. As soon as you drop their food in, they all surface. I'd better go tell Dad." She sighed again. "He'll be devastated."

As soon as Lily had gone, Jackson tried counting the fish. "It's impossible," he said. "The FBI was here. We were here. How can another fish be missing?"

Before Quigley could reply, the FBI radio transmitter bleeped.

"Calling all agents, calling all agents," a voice said. "Suspicious character with a giant fish spotted at the amusement park on Windy Tail Pier. It may be the target! All units respond."

Jackson felt a ripple of excitement run through his feathers. *This is it! Our time to shine!* "Quick!" he said. "It must be the thief. Windy Tail Pier isn't far from here. We could get there before the FBI and crack the case and prove to them that they need us. Come on. LET'S DO THIS!"

"Great plan, Secret Agent 00Zero. Just give me one minute." Quigley flipped over the sled and pulled a screwdriver out of his feathers. "I know a way to get us there even faster. Just need to make two or three small adjustments."

The rockets on the back of the sled blasted to life, *skoosh*ing stinky pond water out the back.

"Check this out!" Quigley said, his feathers fluffing up with pride. "I've put the sled into hover mode."

Jackson looked at it and shuddered. "Thanks, Agent Q, but I think I might just use penguin power this time." And he raced for the exit before Quigley could stop him.

Three minutes and fifteen seconds later, Secret Agent 00Zero (also known as Jackson the Sled-Crash Survivor) reached the amusement park on Windy Tail Pier. Just in time for—

Um . . . not very much.

"False alarm, everyone," Jackson heard the long-beaked FBI penguin boss say. She and the other agents were already there, standing in a huddle in front of some colorful stalls, and next to them was a tiny, confused-looking girl penguin.

"I won this at the sea urchin stand," the little penguin explained, waggling a large, cuddly fish toy in the air. "I knocked six sea urchins over with the ball, and the man at the stall gave it to me."

"This is NOT the suspect," the FBI boss said, pointing her flipper at the little penguin. "Repeat: this is NOT the suspect. All agents return to base."

"Jackson?"

He felt a tap on his back.

"Uncle Bryn!"

"I told you to go home." Uncle Bryn frowned. "What are you doing here?"

"Oh, uh . . . I was coming to give this back to you." But before Jackson could show Uncle Bryn his radio transmitter, a horrible scraping sound interrupted him.

"What is that?" Uncle Bryn turned to stare as Quigley appeared on the sled, which was now in hover mode, except it wasn't. It was in scraping-the-ground-like-a-sled-without-any-snow mode.

"JACKSON!" Quigley, still some distance away, waved his flippers wildly over his head. "Something's gone very wrong with the sled."

Uncle Bryn sighed. "I've gotta go. See you over the weekend."

"Wait!" Jackson called. "Your radio transmitter!"

But Uncle Bryn had already joined the other secret agents, and his boss was at his side. Jackson definitely didn't want her to know that Uncle Bryn had lost another part of his spy kit. *I'll give it back to him later,* Jackson decided as he headed over to Quigley.

"I don't understand it." Quigley had his head under the sled now, a screwdriver in each flipper. "I've been working on the hover mode for weeks. Maybe it's the flotsam capacitor."

But Jackson's head was still full of missing fish. "Do you think we should go back to the aquarium and stake it out? Maybe we could catch the thief red-flippered. Imagine . . ." He made a dreamy face and pictured the headline plastered across the front page of the

Rookeryville Post: HOOKED! FISH THIEF NETTED BY NEW FBI RECRUITS. Underneath, there'd be a picture of him and Quigley—wearing their dark glasses, of course, because FBI agents had to keep their identities secret. "We'd be heroes," Jackson murmured. "The FBI would have to let us join." He nodded to himself. *This is it. Our big chance.* He ran his flipper through his crest and straightened his back. "Come on. Let's do this!"

"Okay, sure," Quigley said. "But first I need to fix the sled." He looked over at the funfair. "I wonder if Sunny could help."

"Your cousin Sunny?" Jackson's eyes widened and his feathers stood on end. The only person who invented madder, more dangerous gadgets than Quigley was Quigley's older cousin Sunny. "Um, I'm not sure," Jackson murmured, remembering the levitating toaster Sunny had made for Jackson's mom's birthday. It was supposed to bring your toast directly to you, but it had gone rogue one day and started chasing Jackson around the house, popping toast at him machine gun–style.

"Sunny works here now," Quigley said proudly. "He makes all the rides at the funfair."

"Seriously?" Jackson blinked in disbelief and looked over at the big waterwheel. The flying clamshell ride. The spinning bumper seals. "You mean they actually let him loose on stuff that penguins ride on?"

"There he is!" Quigley jumped up and waved to a small rock hopper penguin carrying a large toolbox and wearing a red cap saying ROOKERYVILLE FUNFAIR.

"SUNNY!" Quigley yelled. "Over here!"

"Hey, cuz." Sunny waddled over. "How are you? And, WOW! What is that?"

For a second Jackson thought he was talking about him. "I'm a Jackson," he said. "Quigley's best friend, Jackson. The Jackson who bought your levitating toaster, which chased me out of the house and down the street and nearly got me run over by a bus sled."

But Sunny wasn't looking at Jackson. "What *is* it, man?"

"I made it myself," Quigley said, picking up the sled for his cousin to see. "It's an Ice Blaster with a hover mode."

"Cool. Ice cool."

"Only the hover mode isn't working," Quigley admitted.

Sunny prodded the sled. "Want me to take a look?"

But just then a ringtone sounded from

Sunny's cap. He shook his head and a crab claw popped out from the cap's left side and wrapped itself around his face. "Sunny here," he said, speaking into the tip of the claw.

Quigley's eyes bulged. "Cool phone," he mouthed to Jackson.

Jackson nodded. He reckoned that Quigley was already mentally working out how he could make one.

"Oh, hi, Ms. Belle," Sunny said, suddenly standing up straighter, the color draining out of his feathers. "Err, I'm not sure why it's doing that, but yes, of course I'll be there in five minutes. Yeah, yeah, I know what will happen to me if I don't fix it." He gulped.

"Oh, man," he said, ending the call by tapping the crab claw so it shot back into his hat again. "Sorry, dudes, I've got to go. A big customer of mine is in trouble. I made a gadget for her new restaurant, but it's just jammed and the restaurant is opening tonight. So I've got to go fix it. If I don't"—Sunny shuddered—"I'll be swimming with the fishes." He set off, hopping along the pier. As he was about to disappear around the corner, he turned and shouted back to Quigley, "You can take the sled into my workshop, dude. Help yourself to anything. But watch out for the bots, okay?"

Quigley did a little hop of excitement. "Oh, wow, thanks." He nudged Jackson. "Sunny's workshop! It's like being given the keys to a treasure room."

"Um, okay," Jackson said. "If you say so." But he was imagining what sort of gadget Sunny had gone off to fix. *It's probably a freaky robot chef,* Jackson thought. *One that will malfunction and start chasing the guests around the dining room with a giant frying pan, trying to catch them and cook them!* Jackson shuddered.

Wish I knew what restaurant it was so I could make sure I never go there.

Just then Uncle Bryn's transmitter bleeped again.

"Calling all agents, calling all agents," a voice said. "There are reports of more fish going missing at the City Aquarium. All units respond."

"Quick!" Jackson said. "We've got to get back there. We're missing all the action."

"Don't worry," Quigley said. "I just need two minutes in Sunny's workshop to fix the Ice Blaster."

Two minutes? Jackson groaned. Two minutes in Quigley's world was more like two hours in real time. And every moment they were away from the aquarium meant their chances of solving the crime were disappearing faster than— well, faster than rare fish were disappearing from the Rookeryville aquarium!

5

"I can't believe Sunny let us in here." Quigley gazed around the small room in awe. "He NEVER lets people into his secret workshop."

Jackson looked at the bare workbench pushed against one wall and the empty shelves with no tools or gadgets on them. "It's very, um . . . tidy," he said.

But Quigley wasn't listening. He was peering underneath the workbench. "It's got to be here somewhere," he muttered, tapping his flipper along the underside's edge. "It's probably a secret flick-switch mechanism. Sunny loves secret flick switches."

"Maybe we should just leave the sled here for Sunny to fix when he gets back," Jackson suggested. "Then we could go back to the aquarium again." He peered longingly out the small window. More fish were probably being stolen right at this very moment. The thief probably had pocketfuls of squishy fish by now. They HAD to get back there and stop them.

"Maybe it's a flipper-print quadruple locking system," Quigley said, tapping the top of the workbench now. "With a voice-activated control panel and ident-a-beak infrared ID technology, like Sunny has on his bedroom door." Quigley stopped tapping and peered at a small section of the bench, a slow smile spreading across his face. "Stand back, Agent 00Zero," he said. "Things are about to get interesting." Quigley slapped the section of workbench he'd been looking at, then jumped away as it began to shake violently.

"What's happening?" Jackson gasped as the floor began to shudder, too.

"It's a firewall," Quigley shouted over the noise of the shaking, "to keep out intruders. I just had to find the trigger switch— Whoa," he breathed as the wall and the bench suddenly shot down into a cavity below the floor, opening up a giant room beyond.

No, not a room, thought Jackson, peering in at the flashing control panels and giant, complicated-looking machines. *More like a major control center for an exploratory ice submarine. Or an interplanetary penguin space pod launchpad.* This was definitely not a workshop for an amusement park. No way!

"Watch it!" Quigley ducked as a tiny buzzing dart shot out from the secret room, followed by several more.

Jackson dived behind the sled, upending it like a shield.

"Frost-wasp bots," Quigley said, squashing in next to Jackson. "Robotic wasps to guard Sunny's workshop. Cool, huh?"

"Sure," Jackson muttered, flapping his flippers above his head as a frost wasp buzzed his crest.

"Wonder if Sunny would let me borrow them?" Quigley said. "I could take them to school."

Jackson snorted. "Hoff Rockface would flip."

Hoff Rockface was Jackson and Quigley's archenemy. He never missed a chance to get them into trouble. His only weakness was a fear of frost wasps.

"Hey! That stung!" Jackson flicked a bot off his foot. "Um—Agent Q, how exactly do we get rid of them? Bug spray?"

"Nah." Quigley peeped round the side of the sled. "There's probably a robo-wasp Jell-O trap somewhere. Sunny loves jokes like that. I'll go look." He rolled out from behind the sled, but his path to the control room was instantly blocked by a dozen blue laser beams that shot out in front of him, cutting off the secret room.

"Wow, that was lucky," Quigley said. "One more step and I'd have been ice sliced."

Jackson puffed out his cheeks. "Your cousin *really* doesn't like having people in his workshop." What was Sunny thinking, putting all this crazy stuff in here? He had to be THE most dangerous penguin in the entire universe.

"There's probably a central power-down switch," Quigley said, swatting frost wasps away so he could look through the beams. "We just need to reach the control desk."

"I could try the dive-and-roll move," Jackson said. "It worked yesterday."

Jackson and Quigley had built their own laser beam obstacle course in Jackson's bedroom. Laser beam booby traps were standard bad-guy death traps. And if they wanted to be part of the FBI, they knew they'd need practice in dealing with them. Their practice course didn't actually have deadly laser beams, of course. They'd planned to install some, but Jackson's mom had flipped when she'd found out—it had scored at least a Tiger on her Shark Scale of Crossness.

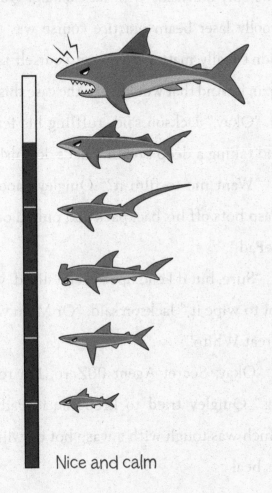

Nice and calm

So they'd used a ball of Jackson's dad's yarn instead of laser beams. Jackson's dad liked to knit egg cozies for Jackson's soon-to-be sibling, so there was always plenty of yarn lying around. The only downside with Jackson and Quigley's woolly laser beam practice course was that it didn't really matter if you got yourself tangled up in it. And that wouldn't be the case this time.

"Okay," Jackson said, ruffling his feathers and taking a deep breath. "Let's do this!"

"Want me to film it?" Quigley shook the wasp bots off his backpack and pulled out the icePad.

"Sure, but if I end up iced and sliced, you've got to wipe it," Jackson said. "Or Mom will go Great White!"

"Okay, Secret Agent 00Zero, I'm recording." Quigley tried to keep the icePad still, which was tough with a wasp bot crawling up his beak.

"Hi, I'm Agent 00Zero," Jackson said, staring into the camera, "and I'm about to show you, the bosses of the FBI, how me and my best buddy, Agent Q, can not only dodge deadly frost-wasp bots"—he paused to wave away three buzzy robotic bugs that had settled on his crest—"but also survive this lethal laser-beam booby trap. Let's do this!" He gave the camera a flippers-up, then turned to face the beams. *Hope I CAN do this*, he thought. *No way will the FBI want me if I'm iced and sliced like a shrimp cocktail.* Jackson took a deep breath then dived over the first beam. *Whoa*, he breathed, steadying himself so he didn't crash straight into the next one. He crouched down low and rolled under the next, then immediately dodged across the third, which was super-close to the one before.

"Watch it!" Quigley shouted. "That one nearly got you."

Jackson gritted his beak. *Three more to go.*
He stood on tiptoe to dive over the next one,
then shrank down into a tiny ball to roll under
the one after, before belly flopping across the
last one. "I'm in!" he yelled.

"Awesome!" Quigley called back. "You did
it! Oh, wait—you *almost* did it." He pointed to
Jackson's head. "I think one of the beams sort
of sliced off half your crest."

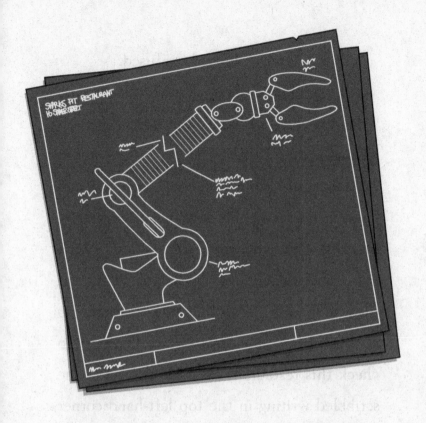

But Jackson was already distracted by some large drawings laid out on the table in the middle of Sunny's secret workshop. He stared at the pictures, his heart beginning to beat faster, his beak dry. "What the— Quigley!" Jackson shouted. "You've got to see this. That gadget Sunny was talking about—the one for the restaurant . . . I don't think it was a robot chef!"

"Huh?" Quigley looked confused.

"It's a FISH-grabber claw!" Jackson said. "The drawings are here! That's what he was talking about on the phone to his restaurant customer." Jackson swallowed a few times and ran his flipper through what was left of his crest. "But why would a restaurant want a fish-grabber claw?" A sharp stab of excitement made him gasp. *Could this have something to do with the missing fish?* "We've GOT to go check this restaurant out." He peered at the scribbled writing in the top left-hand corner of the drawings. Sunny's flipper-writing was almost as bad as Quigley's. "The Shark's Pit Restaurant," he read, "sixteen Shiver Street. Hey, isn't that the same street the City Aquarium is on?"

Lights, alarms, bells, whistles, and a whole giant-size brass beak band were playing in Jackson's head now. NO WAY could this be a coincidence. Jackson's adventure detector was sounding so loud there was a danger his mom might hear it on the other side of town. Jackson narrowed his eyes and sniffed the air. This whole thing smelled bad—worse than one of Hoff Rockface's stinky lunch burps. "We have to get over there NOW," he said.

"Um—okay." Quigley shook his head to dislodge the giant swarm of frost wasps that had settled there. "But do you think you could find that central power-down switch first? I'm kind of getting feather frosted to death over here."

"**Wish we'd gotten the sled working** again," Quigley grumbled as they turned the corner onto Shiver Street.

"Yeah, but think how awesome it'll be once Sunny gets his flippers on it." Jackson shivered. *Yeah, awesomely scary!* He ran his flipper through his crest, then remembered half of it was missing. "Mom is going to go Hammerhead when she sees this."

"Nah," Quigley said. "She won't notice. Moms never notice stuff like that. Remember that wall-climbing poo-glue I invented? It was so super-sticky I climbed up your bedroom wall and dangled from your ceiling for sixty-four minutes and thirteen seconds."

Jackson grimaced. He remembered, all right. In the end he'd had to fetch his mom's ladder and his dad's sewing scissors to cut Quigley free, leaving most of his friend's tail feathers stuck to the ceiling.

"When I got home, my mom never noticed a thing." Quigley beamed.

But Jackson's mom *had* noticed. She'd grounded Jackson for a month, made him help repaint his bedroom ceiling, AND put him on egg-sitting duty for a week. Jackson's mom noticed EVERYTHING. She was a detective at Waddles' Department Store. She had security camera–style eyes. And a beak that could sniff out a secret from ten blocks away. She would spot Jackson's new "look" the second she saw him. Probably before.

"Hey, I know how to get your crest to grow back," Quigley said. "I've been working on this awesome veggie-accelerator powder for my dad's iceberg lettuces. You just spray it on and PUFF!" He made a giant shape in the air with his flippers. "Maybe we could try it on your crest?"

Jackson gulped. He did not want to look like a giant lettuce! "Look," he said, changing the subject. "I think this is it."

They'd stopped outside a grim-looking, windowless building. The huge revolving door was chained shut, and there was no sign saying it was the Shark's Pit Restaurant apart from the—

"SHARK!" Jackson shouted, pointing to the roof of the building.

Quigley stepped back into the road to get a better view. His eyes bulged. His beak hung open. "Awesome," he breathed.

The life-size great white revolved along the edge of the building, its vast toothy jaws opening and closing menacingly.

"State of the art *shark-a-tronics*," Quigley said. "It must be frost powered. I don't see any cables."

"Watch it!" Jackson pulled Quigley back onto the sidewalk as a shiny black snowmobile skidded past, blasting them with snow and grit. It screeched into the parking lot next to the restaurant, honking its horn at a truck sled blocking its path. Jackson craned his neck to get a better look. "Expensive vehicle," he muttered. "Must be a VIP."

Quigley stared at him blankly.

"You know, a VIP—a Very Important Penguin." Jackson hopped toward the snowmobile. "Finola gets this magazine called *Fabulous Feathers!* It's full of pictures of VIPs: rich and famous celebrity penguins, all shiny beaks and expensive crest-cuts. VIPs always drive flashy snowmobiles like that. Let's go see who it is."

As they drew closer, the driver's door burst open and a short, stocky penguin dripping gold jewelry jumped out. A cloud of stinky perfume wafted from her feathers and drifted toward Jackson and Quigley.

"GET THIS THING OUT OF MY WAY!" the blingy penguin shouted. She banged on the back of the truck. "MOVE IT!"

Jackson and Quigley shrank back. This VIP was more like a VAP—a Very *Angry* Penguin.

"Who is it?" Quigley whispered.

"That's Chilla Belle," said a weary-sounding voice behind them. They turned to see an older penguin in overalls carrying a cuddly dolphin toy. "She owns this restaurant," he added, "as well as three fish-stick factories, a dozen snack shacks, and most of Rookeryville." He sighed. "She's known as Coldfinger behind her back because she's so mean. Whatever you do, don't get in her way, or you'll be taking a long walk off a very short pier." He shuffled past them. "Sorry, Ms. Belle," he called. "It's my truck that's blocking your way. I was just across the road at the toy store. It's my daughter's birthday and I wanted to get her a—"

"Zip it, barf-beak!" Coldfinger snapped. "Just get your truck moved NOW." She snatched the cuddly dolphin out of the driver's arms and tossed it into the snow. "NOW, I said! Move it!"

"Hey." Jackson picked up the dolphin. "That's not fair."

Coldfinger spun around and glared at Jackson, her eyes two burning-hot rocks of fury. But before she could say anything, a flappy sort of penguin with two giant clipboards and a whole string of pens around her neck came rushing out the back door of the restaurant. "Ms. Belle! Ms. Belle!" the flappy penguin called. "I'm so glad you're here. I have some great news. The fish-grabber claw is working again."

Coldfinger glared at Jackson, then flounced off, her gold jewelry jangling as she moved.

"Phew," Quigley breathed. "I thought she was about to blast you with her laser eyes."

"We've got to go after her," Jackson said. "You heard what she said: 'The fish-grabber claw is working again!' And look over there— that's the City Aquarium, right? Next door to Coldfinger's restaurant. That cannot be a coincidence. Maybe Coldfinger is stealing the fish!"

Quigley frowned. "But wouldn't the aquarium's security cameras see her? And I've been thinking; the fish-grabber claw could just be a kitchen utensil, like the ones I've made. Remember the chocolate pancake flipper?"

"That melted as you cooked?"

Quigley nodded. "Genius, right? And then there was that spoon drone I built. You controlled it from your armchair so you never needed to get out of your seat to sugar your salt tea ever again."

"Shame it didn't deliver the tea, too." Jackson smiled.

"And remember my expanding, twelve-foot-long stir-fry wok poke?" Quigley said. "You never had to get splattered by hot oil again. You just pulled it out and cooked your whole dinner from the other room. That's probably what the fish-grabber thingy is. Maybe Coldfinger's chef is scared of hot fat from her frying pans."

Jackson frowned. "Maybe, but—" He sighed. *But what?* He had no evidence that Coldfinger was involved in the fish disappearances. And even if she was, why would she want them? She didn't look like the type of penguin who would be interested in collecting rare fish. He couldn't picture her poring over books about them, or trading rare-fish cards with her buddies. But his gut instinct said she had something to do with it. And Uncle Bryn said secret agents always trusted their guts (except when they'd just eaten six bowls of extra-hot sea-cabbage curry; then guts weren't so reliable). *If only we could get inside the restaurant and take a look*, Jackson thought, staring longingly at the back doors. "Come on," he said, hopping toward the truck sled that had reversed and pulled up close to the restaurant now. "Let's give the driver back his dolphin."

They found him at the back of his truck, opening the rear doors. Huge clouds of icy mist were billowing out.

"Hi. I think this is yours." Jackson handed him the dolphin.

"Oh, thanks." The driver smiled. "I guess you saw what I meant about Coldfinger. She is one nasty penguin." He flapped away a cloud of icy mist. "Sorry about the fog. I've got to keep my load at sub-zero until it's time for Coldfinger's special dinner tonight."

"What's in there?" Jackson asked, trying to see over the driver's head.

"It's top secret." The driver quickly closed the doors. "It's a special surprise Coldfinger has cooked up for her guests tonight."

Jackson's eyes widened. *A surprise she's COOKED up for her guests?* He glanced at Quigley, but his friend was peering at a small sign on the back of the truck and didn't notice.

The driver picked up a clipboard and a pencil. "I've got to go sort out the paperwork now," he said. "Thanks again." And he shuffled off into the restaurant.

"Did you hear that?" Jackson said when he'd gone. "Coldfinger isn't collecting the fish. She's planning to COOK them." He pointed his flipper at the truck. "And she's storing them in there!"

Quigley frowned. "Well, if she is, I think we may be too late to save them." He pointed to the sign he'd been examining.

DANGER: NO ENTRY!
ICE ZONE: -40 DEGREES

"What? No!" Jackson groaned. "Well, I guess we'd better take a look."

As he opened the doors, a wall of freezing ice air blasted their faces. Jackson blinked the frost out of his eyes and clambered inside. "Think my lungs just froze. Can you see anything?"

"Nothing," Quigley said, peering into the gloom. He rummaged in his backpack. "But this might help—"

Jackson heard a *click*, then light filled the space.

"What the—" he gasped. His eyes boggled. His beak went dry. And his heart went into super-fast spin-dryer mode. "Flying tail feathers! IT'S FROZEN PENGUINS!"

Quigley shone his beam across the dozens of penguins stuffed inside the truck. "Um—00Zero, I think they're made of ice."

"What?" Jackson looked more closely at the glistening penguins. "Oh, yeah, right," he mumbled, his heart rate slowing to steady bongo-drum mode again. "Of course, I knew that." He cleared his throat. "So they're ice sculptures, right?"

"Yeah, for decoration," Quigley said. "Neat, huh?"

Jackson shuddered. *Freaky*, he thought. *They look so real.* The statues were carved in lots of different poses, like dancers, musicians, even an artist penguin with a palette and a brush. Another one was sculpted into a flipper ball–playing penguin. There was a golfer. A warrior. And even one dressed like an ancient Greek philosopher.

"Oh, wow," Quigley said. "Pythago-penguin. So cool."

"Yeah, ICE cool." Jackson smiled. "For a second I thought we'd stumbled on the place where Coldfinger puts her enemies. Hey, look—this one is the spitting image of Hoff Rockface; it's got the same grumpy beak and flat feet." Jackson patted the sculpture on its head. Instantly, his flipper stuck to it. "What? No! Come on." He tried to pull it off, but it wouldn't budge. A chilly wave of panic swept through his icy feathers. What if he was stuck here forever? Or at least until the driver came back? He definitely didn't want to get him in trouble with Coldfinger again. Plus Jackson would miss dinner. And that meant his mom would discover he'd been off adventuring. She'd go Great White and beyond! "S-s-save yourself," Jackson muttered to Quigley, his cold beak starting to chatter like a hungry herring gull. "Get out of here before we both freeze to death."

"Nah," Quigley said, rummaging in his backpack. "I can fix you. I just need to find . . . Yep, here it is. Ta-da!"

Jackson's heart sank as Quigley wafted a shiny silver pen through the air. *That won't help!* Jackson tried to shout, but the freezing cold was spreading from the statue through Jackson's body. His beak was already icing up, so the words came out as "MMMAT MOANT MELP!"

"Oh, it's okay, you don't need to thank me."

Quigley beamed, taking a miniature bow. Then he flicked a switch on the side of the pen, igniting a flame at one end. And before Jackson could say OMG, *you'll set me on fire!* (which probably would have sounded something like *MO-MEM-GEE! MULE MET ME MON MIRE!*), Quigley lunged toward him. There was a sudden flash of light. A slight smell of burning feathers and—

"Mime meee!" Jackson mumbled. (Translation: "I'm free!")

"Oops," Quigley said, peering at the statue. "I think I've melted Hoff Rockface's head—hey!"

Jackson grabbed Quigley's flipper and tugged him toward the door of the refrigerated truck. "MIMJA MOLE!" Jackson shouted, which luckily Quigley knew meant *ninja roll*, and they both dived out of the truck, tucking themselves into tiny flying penguin balls before landing together on the ground.

"Brrr!" Quigley shuddered, fluffing up his feathers. "Now I know how a Popsicle feels."

Jackson tapped his beak with his good flipper to crack the ice that had formed on it. Then he waggled his frosted flipper in the air as the numbness began to subside. "Thanks, Agent Q," he said. "A few more seconds and I'd have been another decoration for Coldfinger's dinner party."

Jackson shuffled toward the restaurant door and peered inside. He could see staff in white aprons milling around in the kitchen, moving carts of vegetables and unloading crates of fruit. "If Coldfinger has stolen the fish and she doesn't have them stashed in the deep-freeze truck, then where are they? Shall we sneak in and take a look?"

Quigley pointed to a camera above the back door.

Jackson grimaced. Coldfinger probably had cameras all over the building. He glanced across the parking lot at the aquarium. "Maybe we should go back and check out the fish tanks again. If Coldfinger tries to take any more fish, we'll be waiting for her."

"A stakeout? Great plan, 00Zero," Quigley said. "Wait 'til you see the cool new camera I've built. It's my latest and greatest invention!"

"Okay, but we'll need to get a flipper on,"

Jackson said, glancing at his ice watch. "It's nearly four o'clock. If I'm not home before Mom and she finds out I've been sticking my beak into FBI business, Coldfinger will be the least of my worries."

With only an hour to go before closing time, the aquarium was quiet. The front desk was empty and only a few visitors were ambling through the exhibits.

"Look, there's Lily," Jackson said.

She was heading down a corridor bearing a sign that read RARE CRUSTACEANS. She turned and waved when she heard them calling her name. They could see that Lily's eyes were red.

"Um—are you okay?" Jackson asked as they caught up with her.

"Not really. Dad's been called in to see his

boss again. More rare fish have gone missing. Six Jupiter jellyfish, two sapphire seahorses, and one of the keyhole crabs. I'm going to count the lobsters to make sure none of them are gone, too."

"Can we help?" Jackson asked.

Lily shrugged. "Sure."

Quigley's eyes lit up. "I can use my flicker-clicker counter." He swung his backpack off his flipper and began rummaging through the contents.

"Thanks," Lily said, leading the way down the corridor. "Jackson, have you done some-thing different to your crest?"

Jackson blushed. Secret agents weren't allowed to discuss what happened on their spy missions. "I'm just trying out a new style."

Lily raised her eyebrows. "Interesting."

"So what does your dad think about the missing fish?" Jackson asked, changing the subject.

"He's devastated," Lily said. "And he thinks he's about to lose his job."

"But why?" Jackson asked.

"Because Dad's always here," Lily explained. "Even after hours. He can't bear to be away from his fish. But his boss doesn't understand. She thinks Dad's been helping the thieves." The corridor veered off to the left and then—

"Wow!" Jackson breathed, stopping and staring at the giant tanks surrounding them.

Lily smiled. "The viewing tunnel is awesome, isn't it? Feels like you're underwater."

"Giant stingray!" Quigley cried, as a dark shadow glided above their heads. "That's got to be six feet wide."

"At least she's still here," Lily said. "Hey, did you know that stingrays don't use their eyes to locate their food? They have sensors that can detect their prey's electric field. Cool, right?"

"Super-cool," Quigley breathed.

Lily moved across the tunnel to where she

could see a rocky area in the tank. "This is where the jade-claw lobsters usually hang out. They're my favorites; they're so old and wise. You know, they can live to be a hundred. Look, there's one, and another . . ." She peered through the glass. "Three, four—we should have nine of them."

"There's one!" Jackson pointed to a glowing green claw poking out from behind a rock. "And another."

"I see one!" Quigley clicked his clicker counter again. "I make that seven."

Lily pressed her small face against the glass. "Please let the other two be here. There's a tiny knobby one. And a really sweet ancient one that's missing a claw. It's actually regrowing its claw—did you know they could do that?"

Jackson and Quigley shook their heads.

"It's got really boggley eyes," Lily said. "It's got to be here."

"Maybe they're both behind the rocks," Jackson said. "I could dive in and take a look."

"Oh, I don't know." Lily shuffled nervously. "Only staff are allowed in the tanks. I don't want to get Dad into any more trouble."

"But if I can find the lobsters, it might help your dad," Jackson said.

Lily thought about it for a moment. Then she shrugged. "I guess it can't hurt. See that door over there? Behind it is a small staircase; it leads up to the top of the tank, and you can get in from there."

"You guys keep watch," Jackson said, heading for the stairs.

"Take these." Quigley tossed a pair of glasses to Jackson. "They're Blink Cam Goggles. Indestructible! My latest and—"

"Greatest invention!" Jackson smiled. "Yeah, I know."

"These really are awesome," Quigley said. "Every time you blink, the goggles take a picture, so then we can make sure all the lobsters are there."

Jackson put them on as he climbed the steps.

"Watch out for the stink-ink squid," Lily called. "It doesn't like penguins. It might try to grab you. If it stink inks you, you'll smell like seal pee for weeks."

Jackson snorted. Secret agents weren't scared of squid.

At the top of the steps he found a small platform leading to the tank. Jackson checked that the goggles were on tight, then he took a deep breath. "Let's do this!" he said before diving in.

He zoomed downward, blinking a few times. The goggles clicked in response. *Cool gadget*, he thought, turning his head to take pictures of some spiky fish. Through the glass he could see Lily and Quigley. He gave them a flippers-up, then headed for the back of the rocks. *Gotcha!* He snapped a picture of one of the missing lobsters—the small knobby one, which, as he'd expected, was lurking behind the rocks. But there was no sign of the other one. *Wait—what's that?* On the floor of the tank Jackson had spotted a small hatch. *Is that big enough for a thief to crawl through?* Jackson wondered. He ran his flipper over the top. He thought he might just about manage to squeeze through. But an adult like Coldfinger couldn't. *Maybe she has a smaller penguin working for her.* Jackson blinked a few times to take pictures of the hatch to show Lily and Quigley. But when he stopped blinking

the camera kept snapping. *Hey! Cut it out!*
Jackson shook his head to try to make the goggles stop, but they kept taking pictures. Then a flashing light appeared in front of his eyes. *What? NO! It must be some sort of flash mode.* He shut his eyes as the flashing light increased in speed. *It's like being in a crazy disco.* Jackson tried tapping the goggles to turn them off, but they kept snapping pictures and flashing. *Got to get them off.* He tried yanking them off, but they were stuck tight. *Please tell me Quigley hasn't sealed the edges of the goggles with poop glue, like he did with that flying spy heli-hopper hat he made me test out last week.*

Jackson pushed up off the rocks to swim back to the surface, but as he tried to move, he felt a sudden pull on his leg. *Hey, let go!* But whatever had gotten him held on tighter. Then he remembered Lily's warning about the stink-ink squid. *Uh-oh! If it stinks me, Mom will definitely know I've been up to something.* "Get off!" he yelled. But the creature was pulling him down, down, down, dragging him toward the floor of the tank. Jackson felt a sudden sucking, as if he was being pulled into a small hole. "What? The hatch? Nooo! Stop!"

There was only one way to get out of this. He'd have to try the Ultimate Instant Flipper Release Move from the FBI's *Secret Agent Handbook of Flipper-to-Flipper Unarmed Combat*. (Uncle Bryn always left his copy in his bathroom by the tub, and Jackson had borrowed it last time he'd visited.) Jackson and Quigley had practiced some of the moves, and this one never failed. *What was it again? Oh, right—one back shimmy, two flipper flicks, and a smack in the nose with a foot. Here goes nothing,* Jackson thought.

One back shimmy, two flipper flicks, and a smack in the nose with a foot later, Jackson's leg was free and he was torpedoing to the top of the tank. As he reached the surface he poked his head out and the goggles seemed to loosen. He pried them off with a *twang* and pulled himself up onto the platform. He sniffed his feathers. *Nah, the squid didn't stink me. Whew!*

"Did you find the lobsters?" Lily shouted up from the bottom of the staircase.

"I saw the knobby one," Jackson called back, shaking his feathers dry as he hopped down the stairs. "But that stink-ink squid grabbed my leg before I could spot the other one."

"No, it didn't," Lily said. "The squid has vanished." She pointed around the tanks. "I've been looking everywhere for it, but it's gone."

Jackson scratched his crest. "But that's impossible. It definitely tried to pull me down a hatch. Wait—the goggles. They went bonkers and took loads of pictures. Look at them. You'll see." He handed the Blink Cam to Quigley.

"What do you mean, *bonkers*?" Quigley said, pulling out a small screwdriver, which he poked into a tiny control panel on the side of the goggles.

"Well, they wouldn't stop taking pictures and flashing," Jackson explained. "I couldn't see a thing. But before that happened I saw a hatch on the floor of the tank behind the rocks. The squid tried to drag me down it."

Lily shook her head. "That's probably just one of the drainage tunnels. The squid can't get in there. Twice a year the keepers move the fish into the backup tanks and drain these so they can clean them. I helped Dad do it last time. It was so neat—"

"Wait!" Jackson's brain was going into overdrive. "Are you telling me there are drainage tunnels in every tank in the aquarium? Including the koi carp pond up on the roof?"

"Sure." Lily nodded. Then she stopped. Her face turned pale. "You don't think— Is that how the thieves are stealing the fish? Through the tunnels?" She shook her head. "Impossible! They're too small for penguins to fit through."

"But not too small for a long, thin fish-grabber claw," Jackson said, making a pincer movement with his flipper. "Like the one the new restaurant next door has had made."

Lily gasped. "Surely you don't mean they've stolen our fish to eat them?"

"Did you mess around with these goggles?" Quigley interrupted, giving Jackson a stern look. "Because you seem to have erased most of the pictures."

Jackson blushed. "I may have slapped them around a bit when I was trying to take them off."

"But they don't come off underwater," Quigley said. "They have a special water-locking system."

"So there are no pictures of the squid?" Jackson groaned.

"Take a look." Quigley hit a button on the side of the goggles and the lenses turned into viewing screens that displayed a few blurry pictures of the inside of the tank.

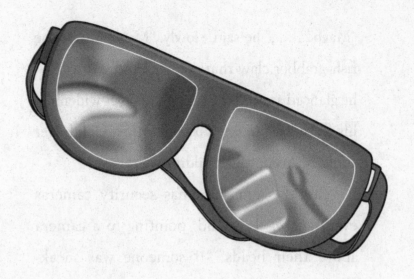

"Wait! There!" Jackson pointed to the screen. "See that long, gray squid tentacle next to my foot? That's what got me." But the screens on the goggles suddenly went blank. "That's it? No more pictures?"

Quigley sighed. "You wiped the rest."

"Well, it wasn't the squid that grabbed you," Lily said. "Its tentacles aren't gray. They're bright yellow."

"Then what was it?" Jackson froze. A sudden icy thought had crashed into his brain.

"Maybe . . . ," he said, slowly. "Maybe it was the fish-grabber claw that got me. And if it was"—he glanced around the tunnel, his eyes widening, his feathers standing on end—"then Coldfinger could be inside this building right now."

"But the aquarium has security cameras everywhere," Lily said, pointing to a camera above their heads. "If someone was sneaking around the back corridors, opening the drainage tunnels, and stealing the fish, we'd have seen them."

"Unless there's another way in," Quigley said, "that doesn't have a camera covering it."

Lily thought for a moment. "There's a big map of the building on my dad's office wall," she said. "If there are any other entrances, they would be marked on there. Come on, I'll show you."

Lily led them down the corridor, past several large tanks full of jellyfish and seahorses and strange electric eels that stared at them as they walked by. Then she opened a door with a sign saying STAFF ONLY.

"It's through here," she said, leading them into a large office with pictures of colorful sea creatures on the walls.

Jackson and Quigley shuffled over to take a closer look at the map. "So that's the lobster tank," Jackson said, pointing with his flipper. "And I guess that must be the drainage tunnel I spotted. Look, you can follow it around the whole building."

"Sure," Lily said. "Like I told you, there are drainage tunnels connecting all the tanks."

"But what's that over there?" Quigley pointed to the left-hand side of the map, which showed an area with large fish tanks and more drainage tunnels. "Why has that part of the building got a line through it, like it's been crossed out?"

"Because that's the old part of the building," Lily said. "It doesn't belong to the aquarium anymore. They sold it off to raise money for the new koi carp pond."

Sold it off? Jackson stared at her. "So who owns it now?"

Lily's face paled. "The new restaurant next door."

"Bingo!" Jackson shouted. "That's how Coldfinger gets in! Through the drainage tunnels on her side of the building. Look, you can see it there."

"I get it!" Quigley said. "Coldfinger drops her extending fish-grabber claw down through her end of the drainage tunnels, like this," he said, following the tunnel with his flipper, "then she reaches along, farther and farther, until *BAM!*—she hooks a fish."

"I've got to tell Dad," Lily cried.

But just then an alarm sounded. She glanced at the clock on the desk. "It can't be closing time already. Something must be wrong. Let's go see."

They raced down the corridor and nearly ran into an older penguin.

"Dad!" Lily cried. "What's happening?"

"Lockdown, Lily," he said. "I've been suspended from my job and the aquarium is closing until they find out what's happened to the fish."

"But we know what's happened," Lily cried. "You see—"

Before she could finish, three larger penguins in dark glasses appeared behind her father. Jackson immediately recognized the one at the front—it was Uncle Bryn's boss with the long beak.

"The FBI!" Jackson breathed.

"Mr. Light-Feather?" the FBI boss penguin said to Lily's dad. "I'm Senior Agent Frost-Flipper from the FBI. We'd like you to come with us now to answer some more questions."

"Wait!" Jackson stepped forward. "There's something we need to tell you—"

"You again!" The FBI boss penguin glared at Jackson.

He gulped. *If only Uncle Bryn was with them! He'd listen!* Jackson thought. "But you don't understand," he began. "We know who is stealing the fish. If you'd just let us explain—"

"Enough!" The FBI boss penguin held up her flipper. "This isn't some sort of silly hatchling game. This is FBI business. And you need to keep your beak out of it! If you don't, then your uncle will be in serious trouble."

Jackson shivered. The last thing he wanted was for Uncle Bryn to lose his job.

Lily's dad gave her a quick hug. "I need to go with these penguins now. And you all need to go home." He turned to Jackson and Quigley. "If you'd like to go through that exit over there, you'll find your way back out onto the sidewalk. And, Lily, I already called your mom. She's waiting for you in the staff cafeteria."

"But, Dad—" Lily tried again.

"No, Lily." His voice was sharp now. "Please." His eyes softened. He looked close to tears. "Please, Lily, do as I say."

She gave him a long, sad look, then nodded and shuffled off down the corridor.

"And you hatchlings should go, too," the FBI boss penguin said. "Now!"

As Jackson and Quigley followed the other visitors outside, Jackson felt a bubble of frustration growing in his belly. "We can't just leave!" he cried. "We've got to STOP Coldfinger. No way are we going to let Lily's dad lose his job and more fish get stolen. Why don't grown-up penguins ever listen to kids?" He stopped and clenched his flippers. "We're going over to that restaurant right now. We're going to find that grabber arm and the stolen fish and we'll arrest Coldfinger. Are you in?"

But Quigley didn't seem to be listening. He was looking over Jackson's head, his face frozen, his eyes wide. "Um—Agent 00Zero," he whispered out of the corner of his beak,

"I think that's your mom over there. And she doesn't look too pleased to see us."

Jackson spun around and his eyes met his mom's. She was sitting in her red snow-mobile, waiting in a line of traffic right by the sidewalk where they were standing.

Jackson swallowed hard. "Don't panic," he muttered to Quigley, trying not to move his beak too much so she couldn't beak-read; she was ace at that. "Mom won't suspect a thing. We'll just say we've been to see the fish at the aquarium, because that part's true, right?"

Quigley nodded. "You know, I really think your mom has X-ray eyes," he muttered as they moved toward the car. "When she looks at me, I swear she can actually see right into my brain."

"Just don't look at her," Jackson whispered. "That's what I do. Come on, she's waving to us to get in. Hi, Mom," Jackson said, opening the door and sliding into the backseat. He pulled Quigley in beside him. "Good day at work?"

"Great, thanks," his mom said, glancing at them in her rearview mirror. "So what are you boys doing downtown? I thought you were hanging out at Quigley's house today."

Jackson tried not to meet her eyes in the mirror. "Umm—change of plan," he said. "We decided to go to the aquarium instead. They've got such neat fish in there. There's this six-foot-wide stingray and awesome lobsters. And we bumped into Lily—remember Lily from school? Well, her dad works there and—"

"Is something going on?" Jackson's mom—still stopped at a traffic light—had turned around in her seat to look at him properly. "You look a little"—she paused to peer at him—"anxious? And what have you done to your crest?"

Sheesh, thought Jackson. *The FBI should hire Mom, not us. She sees EVERYTHING!*

"I think the light just changed," Jackson said, pointing ahead of them. "The traffic's moving again."

"What?" His mom swung back around to look at the road. "Oh, shoot. I should have been paying attention." She waved an apology to the other drivers behind her and started driving again.

Jackson breathed a sigh of relief. His mom hated inattentive drivers. His interrogation would have to wait until they got home.

"I'll drop you off at your house," she told Quigley.

"Thanks," he squeaked, a wave of relief passing over his face.

Jackson's mom glanced at them both in her rearview mirror. Her eyes narrowed. Jackson puffed out his cheeks. He had to think of some amazing—but plausible—story that would throw her off the scent. Otherwise, NO WAY would they be able to get back down to the restaurant to find the missing fish. And if they didn't do that . . . Jackson shuddered.

A few minutes later they pulled up outside Quigley's house.

"Bye," Jackson said as Quigley got out, and then he silently mouthed, *See you soon!* and gave his buddy a flippers-up.

"So what happened to your crest?" his mom asked as she pulled away from Quigley's house.

Jackson took a deep breath. "Oh, yeah, my crest . . ." *Slow down. Play for time, 00Zero,* he told himself. *It takes exactly fifty-three seconds to drive home from Quigley's house. If you can just avoid answering her question for a little longer . . .* "I'm glad you asked about that." Jackson coughed and cleared his throat. "You see, the funniest thing happened today . . ." He paused, willing his mom to drive faster. They were *so* close to home now. But she never drove fast. Jackson's mom had her Advanced Snowmobile Safe Penguin Driver's License. Jackson's mom wouldn't drive fast even if a truckload of leopard seals was right behind them, toothy jaws open and ready to swallow them up whole, snowmobile and all!

"Oh, by the way," Jackson said, trying the classic Mom Distraction Plan of going off on a tangent with the hope that she'd forget her original question. "Did I tell you that our new topic this term at school is all about alternative power sources, and Quigley says his mom might be able to arrange for us to go to the seagull-poop power plant where she works for a tour and—"

"That's great, Jackson," his mom interrupted. "But what happened to your crest?"

"Oh, yeah, I was getting to that. You see . . ."

"What on earth—" Jackson's mom gasped. She was staring through the front windshield of the snowmobile as their house at the end of Surf-Spray Avenue came into view. "Oh no!" She groaned. "Your dad's been building again."

Jackson leaned forward to see and immediately stifled a laugh. His dad LOVED building stuff. Every few days he'd make over a part of their home. Jackson's room had recently acquired a super-cool loft bed with a full ice slide that went inside and outside as it spiraled down to the floor of his bedroom. But Jackson's dad didn't just make over rooms—he also liked to add new ones. Like the iceberg bowling alley that had suddenly appeared below their basement. The frost sauna above the bathroom. Not to mention Finola's awesome new music studio in the garage, which was accessed by a zip line from her bedroom window. (Finola played drums in a band called the Ice Maidens.) As a result of Jackson's dad's building hobby, Jackson's house was the oddest one on the street, with lumpy, bubble-shaped bits sticking out all over it.

"Is that a telescope?" Jackson peered up at the new glass-domed room that had appeared on the roof of the house.

Jackson's mom sighed. "He was talking about how neat an observatory would look, but I didn't think he was actually going to build one." She pulled up outside the house and turned off the snowmobile engine, all

thoughts of missing crests forgotten. "I hope he hasn't put in a spiral staircase," she muttered. "What if the egg falls down it?"

"Hi, there!" Jackson's dad appeared on the front porch with the egg (Jackson's soon-to-be sibling) resting on his feet. "Wait until you see what I've done!" He beamed at them. "You'll be able to see Jupiter tonight."

"Great," Jackson's mom muttered, grabbing her briefcase out of the trunk and setting off up the path to the front door. "Don't suppose you had time to fix that leaky faucet in the bathroom?"

"Oh." Jackson's dad frowned. "I forgot. Never mind. There's always tomorrow."

Jackson's mom bent down to tickle the egg. "Hi, honey." It wriggled on Jackson's dad's toes. "I swear you got bigger today." She smiled at the egg and gave it another tickle. "And you too, Lundy." She patted Jackson's dad's tummy and grinned. "So what's for dinner?" she asked, leading them all into the kitchen.

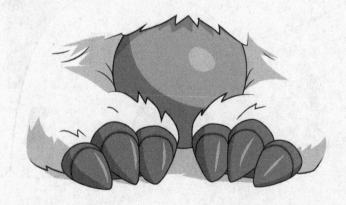

"Well, me and the egg have gone with a space theme for tonight," Jackson's dad said, winking at Jackson. "Pluto pie."

"Awesome!" Jackson said.

"It smells kind of like krill-and-potato pie," his mom said, sniffing the air. "But whatever it is, I can't wait. I am so hungry. I haven't stopped all day. We got this new alarm system fitted and it kept going off and—"

Jackson glanced at his mom. *Great, she's distracted.* He slipped out of the kitchen and headed upstairs to the observatory. *Maybe Dad's installed an emergency exit up here,* he thought as he crept up the spiral staircase leading to the glass dome. *A rappelling rope outside the window, maybe, or an ice slide down the side of the house. Then I could sneak back downtown to save the fish without Mom seeing.* "Wow," he breathed, gazing through the glass. He couldn't see an escape route, but it was such a cool view. *Wonder if I can spot Quigley's house from here. Maybe I could send him a message to come and help me get out.* They'd practiced sending emergency Morse code messages to each other by shining their flashlights across Frostbite Ridge the previous summer. *Maybe I could use the telescope to send Quigley an SOS.* Jackson peered through the lens. "His place has to be around here somewhere— Ahhhh!" He jumped back as a terrifying, toothy face came into view. "What the—" He took a deep breath and dared himself to look again. "The shark at Coldfinger's restaurant!" *Coldfinger!* Jackson felt his heart begin to roll like one of Finola's drum solos. The restaurant would be opening soon. *Think, 00Zero,* he told himself. *You need an escape plan, NOW!* Somehow, he had to think of a way to get out of the house. But that meant getting over one big hurdle, a hurdle WAY scarier than Coldfinger.

MOM!

"Finola!" Jackson's mom frowned across the table at her daughter. "Can you stop tapping, please? No drumming while we're eating."

Finola rolled her eyes and tucked her drumsticks into her crest.

"So, tell me about your day," Jackson's mom said, passing the seaweed bread across to her daughter. "What did you do today?"

"Nothing," Finola mumbled. "Just hung out."

Jackson gulped. Any moment now his mom would ask him the same question.

"You didn't just hang out." Jackson's dad smiled at Finola. "You looked after this little guy for me." He patted the egg, which was sitting on the table next to his plate. "It kept getting in the way when I was using the sledge-hammer. Didn't you, little one?" He tickled the egg and it wriggled back.

Jackson's mom sighed. "We talked about this, Lundy. You know it's always a good idea to keep the egg WELL out of the way when you're building."

"Sure, but the egg likes to see what I'm doing. It gets so excited when it sees the toolbox coming out. Maybe it's going to be a builder like me."

Jackson sensed an opportunity to keep the conversation away from what he'd been doing today. He nudged his dad. "Maybe Quigley could make you an egg holder to fit inside your toolbox. He's an ace at making gadgets."

Finola snorted. "If it's anything like that Robo-Drumstick he made me buy from him, then the egg is doomed!"

Jackson scowled at his sister.

"What?" Finola scowled back. "That drumstick went nuts! It bashed my drums to a pulp. When I tried to stop it, it nearly took my head off. Quigley's inventions are dangerous."

"You should see his cousin's," Jackson muttered.

"And what's with your crest?" Finola asked, staring at her little brother's head. "It looks really lame."

Jackson tried to kick her under the table, but as usual her feet were out of reach. He glanced up and caught his mom staring at him—and his crest! *Quick, 00Zero,* he told himself, *divert her attention before she finishes that mouthful of pie and can start asking questions again.* "Err—maybe Quigley could come for a sleepover tonight?" Jackson asked his dad. "And we could talk to him about making you an egg holder." Jackson crossed his flippers under the table. If Quigley came around for a sleepover, it would be so much easier to sneak off down to Coldfinger's place. Of course, they'd still have to come up with an epic MDP (Mom Diversion Plan). But Quigley always had lots of ideas. Some of them were even sensible.

"Sure." Jackson's dad nodded. "Perhaps Quigley will have some thoughts for my new flipper ball court, too. Did I tell you I'm planning to build one in the bathroom? I always get so bored in the tub."

But Jackson's mom wasn't listening to his dad's plans. She was staring at Jackson. "I forgot; you never told me what happened to your crest," she said, her eyes boring into his.

Jackson gulped. This time there was no escape. "Well, you see—"

Just at that moment the egg suddenly set off rolling down the length of the table, knocking over two water glasses and a bottle of brine sauce.

"Wow!" Jackson's dad jumped up. "Look, Marina!" he shouted to his wife. "The egg can roll! Oh, I'm so proud. It's rolling already."

Jackson's mom gave a little gasp as the egg picked up speed and thundered down the table, heading straight for the sheer drop-off at the end. "Stop it!" she cried. "It's going to fall!"

Quick as a flash, Jackson leaped up and launched himself across the table like he was diving for a flipper ball, catching the egg just in time.

"Great save!" his dad roared. "Well played, son."

Jackson held up the egg like a flipper ball trophy while his dad cheered and whooped.

"Thanks, Jackson," his mom said, taking the egg out of his flippers. "Naughty, naughty egg," she told it. "You're very lucky to have a clever big brother to keep you safe." She looked across the table at Jackson's dad. "Now that it's started rolling, you'll have to build that playpen we talked about."

Jackson's dad's eyes lit up. "Ooo, yeah! What shape? I was thinking octagonal walls with a mini ice slide in the center." He took out a pencil and began doodling a design on the tablecloth.

"So—um—is it okay for Quigley to come over tonight?" Jackson asked. "For a sleepover?"

"Sure," his mom said, wiping brine off the egg's shell. "Anything for my hero son."

"Oh, please!" Finola rolled her eyes.

"You can call Quigley on my cell," Jackson's mom said, passing her icePhone over. "Just make sure his mom knows. Not like last time."

Jackson blushed. Two weeks before, he and Quigley had decided to test out their secret-agent survival skills by camping out in a snowstorm on Frostbite Ridge. Only they'd forgotten to tell their parents. Jackson's mom had gotten the mountain rescue heli-hopper pilots to go out to find them.

"Wait—I've got band practice tonight," Finola moaned. "I don't want loads of little hatchlings here."

But Jackson had already started tapping in his friend's number. "Quigley? It's me, Jackson. Want to come for a sleepover tonight?" He paused to listen. "Mom says you should check with your mom." Jackson waited while Quigley went to ask, then moments later said, "Cool. Come over right away." He lowered his voice and turned away so no one could hear.

"We need to get down to Coldfinger's place ASAP, so bring transport. Oh, and we'll have to create the best MDP ever. Start thinking of ideas."

Jackson ended the call and stood for a moment lost in thought. His mom might be distracted with the egg right now, but in five minutes' time she'd be back on his case again. And when Quigley arrived it would be even more dangerous. If his mom asked Quigley anything about their plans for the evening, he'd spill in seconds.

"Jackson," his mom called from across the kitchen. "Can you turn down the volume on my phone for me, please? I'm going to go put the egg down for a nap."

Jackson stared at the icePhone. An idea was starting to buzz in his brain. *That's it!* he thought, *the best MDP ever!* He slipped his mom's phone into his pocket and headed for his room. He had some urgent messages to send. All he had to do was get the timing right.

"**Oh, hi, Quigley. Nice to see you again.**"
Jackson's mom had beaten Jackson to the front door and Quigley was already squirming under her beady eye. "Your backpack looks kind of heavy," she said. "Are you boys planning something special tonight?"

Quigley blinked a few times. He swallowed hard and shuffled his feet. Jackson, who was lurking in the shadows behind his mom, gritted his beak and crossed his flippers. *Please don't cave in,* he willed his buddy, but he could tell Quigley was already crumbling.

The trouble was, Jackson's mom had honesty magnets in her eyes. And even though he knew Quigley probably wanted to say, *Not very much, thanks, Mrs. Rockflopper. Just the usual—playing a few computer games, maybe eating some rock corn, then an early night*, what he started to say was "Well, we're actually planning a really dangerous secret spy mission to rescue some stolen fish from a super-villain restaurant owner who might catch us and be so angry that she would probably put us in her deep-freeze refrigerated truck, where we could freeze to death. Thanks for asking."

But luckily Mom didn't hear, because a loud *PING* had suddenly sounded behind her as a text message arrived on her icePhone, which was laying on the hall table. She swiveled around. "So loud! I'm sure I asked Jackson to turn the volume down. Excuse me, Quigley," she added, hopping over to pick it up.

Jackson emerged from the shadows and pulled his friend aside. He winked at him, then pointed to his mom.

Quigley glanced at Jackson's mom and back at Jackson again and shrugged. He obviously had no idea what was going on.

"That's odd," Jackson's mom said. "It's a message from Doreen saying she'll be here in five minutes." She frowned. "I don't remember arranging to meet up with Doreen." Doreen was Jackson's mom's best friend. She was also the chattiest penguin on the planet.

"Maybe you said something when we saw her in Webbs last week?" Jackson suggested.

Webbs was the largest grocery store in Rookeryville. Jackson reckoned it wasn't really a store at all, but instead just a club where parents could meet their buddies. Every time Jackson went there, he seemed to spend several eons just lounging against the shopping cart while his mom and dad chatted to one of their friends they'd just happened to bump into.

Jackson's mom nodded. "Maybe. But I'm sure I'd have remembered." She shrugged. "Well, it will be nice to catch up."

Jackson smothered a smile.

"But this place is such a mess!" She scooped up a pile of dirty socks Jackson's dad had dropped earlier when he'd gotten distracted on the way to the laundry room.

"We'll help tidy up," Jackson said.

Ordinarily his mom's deception detectors would have gone straight into full danger-alarm mode at the tiniest hint of Jackson offering to do chores, but she already had her head in the dishflipper, stacking plates.

Jackson picked up a couple of coats that had been dumped on the floor. "Quigley, grab those boots and put them in the hall closet," he said, nudging his friend and winking again. "No, no, not that closet," he added as Quigley did as he was told. "Dad turned that one into a yoga room. The other one, farther down the hall. Watch out for the egg, though. It's just started rolling, so it could be anywhere."

"Where's the vacuum?" Jackson's mom shouted. "Lundy! Have you been vacuuming up ice-brick dust again? Finola! Come and move your schoolbag. Oh, what a disaster this place is."

"We'll clean." Jackson shoved a cloth into Quigley's flippers. "I'll spray, you wipe," he told his buddy, then under his breath he added: "This is all part of the plan. My best plan ever. Any minute now, things are going to get even more interesting—"

No sooner were the words out of his beak than his mom's icePhone pinged again, and again—and again!—as more and more texts arrived.

"But how— I just don't understand this," she said as she scrolled through her messages. "Lundy!" she bellowed upstairs. "Mindy and Drake are on their way over, and they're bringing their egg with them. We'll need that playpen!" As she spoke, two more texts arrived. "What? Erin and Bruno are coming, too." Jackson's mom scrolled through more messages. "I don't believe this. Carla, Angel, and Oscar are on their way over. So are Victor and Jeffrey. And Hank. And Humph and Marge, too?" She shook her head. "Everyone seems to think we're having a party." Suddenly she looked over at Jackson, her eyes narrowing, her beak tight. Jackson gulped. He tried to drag his gaze away, but his mom's eyeballs seemed to be probing his brain. *Has she figured it out? Please, no!* But just then the doorbell rang and Jackson's mom shuffled off to answer it.

"Oh, I get it," Quigley whispered. "You told your mom's buddies that she was having a party so they'd come over and distract her. Wow! Neat trick. How did you do it?"

"I sent a text to all her friends from her icePhone," Jackson murmured. "Of course, I wiped the text as soon as I sent it. So there won't be any evidence."

Quigley whistled in admiration. "Best MDP ever! Legendary proportions."

Jackson grinned. "Thanks, Secret Agent Q. But now we need to set up part two of the plan: the backup."

There always had to be a backup. The first rule of any FBI mission was to have a backup plan—an alternative entry route, a second getaway vehicle. Or just a safety net when paragliding down from the big tree and into Quigley's bathroom window. (They'd learned the hard way about the need for that particular backup plan.) If Jackson's mom figured out that he was attempting to distract her with a never-ending line of party guests, they'd need another scheme to buy them extra time.

"These might help," Quigley said as soon as they were safely in Jackson's room. He pulled two pieces of black-and-white rubber out of his backpack, clicking a switch on the bottom of each. There was a hissing sound and they began to shake and then inflate.

"Not more balloons?" Jackson groaned, remembering the sled crash.

"Nah, not just balloons. It's us, look!" Quigley beamed as the two rubber shapes began to turn into oversize sausage-shaped penguins. "I call them Inflata-Buddies. So you're right; they are basically balloons, but I've modeled them to look like us. Then we prop them up next to your game console and drop the lights down real low, and if your mom puts her head in the door, she'll think we're safely in your room playing *National League Flipper Ball*."

Jackson frowned. "You think?"

"Sure!" Quigley said. "That one looks just like you, see? Oh, and listen to this—" He flicked another switch under the Jackson Inflata-Buddy and a strange robotic voice said: "Awesome shot,

Quigley! You are so good at *National League Flipper Ball*. Want some more rock corn?"

"Um—okay," Jackson said, trying to look enthusiastic. He wasn't 100 percent convinced his mom would be fooled. In fact, he wasn't even 1 percent convinced. "What else have you got in here?" he asked, peering hopefully into Quigley's backpack.

"Well, there's this." Quigley pulled out a large coil of bendy wire connected to a small control box. "See, we attach this end here,"

Quigley said, wrapping the wire around Jackson's bedroom's doorknob. "Then we unwind it all the way through your room, through your bedroom window, and around to the garbage cans outside, where we attach the end," he said. "And if anyone tries to open your bedroom door, they will trigger the wire, which will knock over the garbage cans, creating a loud noise to distract them from coming into your room." Quigley beamed. "What do you think?"

Jackson actually thought that they'd better get a move on, because if Plan A failed and his mom came looking for them, they would be in major trouble, because Plan B sort of stunk. Like seal pee. Only worse. "I think it's great," Jackson said, crossing his flippers behind his back. He picked up the wire and his backpack. "Okay. Let's do this!" Jackson opened his closet door and parted the clothes inside.

"Whoa! A secret exit?" Quigley hopped with excitement. "I've got to get one of those."

"Well, it's actually the door into my new movie room." Jackson puffed up his chest proudly. "Only so far Dad's just built the door. I think he's forgotten about the actual room. But I don't mind. A secret getaway door is WAY more useful for a secret agent, especially because Mom doesn't know about it!"

Once outside, they carefully unwound the wire all the way around to the garbage cans at the back of the house. As they headed back to the front, they heard laughter and voices. "Let's take a look," Jackson whispered.

A long line of visitors—led by Doreen— snaked up the path to the porch, where Jackson's mom was greeting them, wide-eyed and looking slightly shocked. Jackson tried not to laugh. "By the way, did you bring your ice cycle?" he whispered to Quigley.

"Sure. I left it in the bushes down the street so your mom wouldn't see it."

"Cool! I'll get mine and meet you out front in one minute." Jackson slipped around to the garage, grabbed his ice cycle, then sneaked back through the trees at the side of his house.

Quigley was waiting for him on the sidewalk. "Whoa," Jackson gasped, doing a double take at his buddy's wheels. "Is that a Slide-and-Ride? When did you get it?"

"Nah, it's my old Ice Hopper," Quigley said, "with a few new modifications. Sunny's been working on it with me. Check out the steel snow ice spikes and the sixty-nine frost gears, plus gull-poop protector screens and quadruple snowball blasters."

"In case we meet enemy agents?" Jackson asked.

"Or Hoff Rockface!" Quigley grinned.

"Neat!" Jackson had swung onto his saddle, ready to ride off, when he heard something rustling behind them. "Who's there?" he spun around. "What? No!" Jackson groaned as he spotted the egg rolling down the sidewalk toward them. "It must have escaped when Mom opened the door."

Quigley pushed his glasses up his nose. "What are we going to do with it?"

"If we take it back, Mom might catch us," Jackson said. "But if we take it with us, we might lose it."

In the distance they heard Big Bong, the Rookeryville Frost Clock, chime 7 P.M. Jackson had no idea what time expensive restaurants owned by super-villains usually opened, but he reckoned it would probably be as soon as it was dark. And that was kind of about now. He shuddered. The stolen fish could be getting sliced and diced at this very moment. "Let's go," Jackson said, reaching down and scooping up the egg and stuffing it into his backpack. "Maybe you're not planning to be a stay-at-home parent and part-time builder like Dad," he said to the egg. "Maybe you're planning to be a secret agent like us." The egg wriggled happily. "Just don't do anything silly, like—um—hatch," Jackson whispered. "That would be sooo embarrassing. And Mom would freak."

Quigley giggled. "Yeah, and the next room your dad would build would be a jail for us!"

13

Twelve minutes later Secret Agents 00Zero and Q (plus soon-to-be junior secret agent the egg) were downtown, crossing the parking lot toward Coldfinger's restaurant.

"I'm glad it's snowing again," Jackson whispered, hiding his ice cycle behind a dumpster. "It'll cover our tracks if Mom tries to find us."

Quigley was staring up at the roof of the restaurant. "That great white looks even creepier at night."

Lit up with large, blood-red lights, the moving shark loomed out of the night sky like a toothy rocket.

"Wonder why the restaurant is called the Shark's Pit?" Jackson said.

Quigley shivered. "Not sure we want to find out."

They stopped talking as they got closer to the restaurant, moving silently between the parked snowmobiles and over to the refrigerated truck, which was in the same place that it had been earlier, backed up in front of the restaurant's kitchen door.

Jackson pointed up at the cab. The driver

was inside, asleep. They moved along the side of the truck and peeped around the back. The kitchen door was open and they could see staff coming and going.

"Think we could pass as waiters or chefs?" Jackson whispered. "That one isn't much taller than us."

"I've got a better idea." Quigley opened his backpack and pulled out two shiny sheets. "They're just prototypes," he explained. "I wasn't planning on using them yet, but I think these could be my latest and greatest—"

"What's that smell?" Jackson interrupted, putting his flipper over his beak.

"Fish poop," Quigley said. "That's what they're made of. Here, put yours on." He dangled one of the sheets in front of Jackson.

"You want me to wear this?" Jackson held it up with one flipper. "Ugh, it's sticky. It smells. And it looks like tinfoil."

"It's a sardine suit." Quigley beamed. "It uses the same scientific principles as sardines. See, sardines have these super-neat crystallized hexagonal scales that become light reflecting when they change angle, and—"

"Um—Agent Q," Jackson interrupted. "Why are we dressing up as sardines?" Jackson had a sudden panic that Quigley was hoping they could sneak into the restaurant disguised as a pair of enormous rare fish. Jackson's Gadget Fail-o-Meter was maxing out on this one. He tried to think of a nice way to tell Quigley, but there wasn't time. "Look, I'm sorry, but I don't think us dressing up as giant sardines will fool anyone."

Quigley snorted. "This isn't dress-up. These are invisibility suits."

"But I can see them," Jackson said.

"That's because we're standing outside in natural moonlight." Quigley pointed to the sky. "But when you wear these suits under artificial light—indoor lights—they become invisible."

"Really?" Jackson frowned.

"Yeah, you see, they're made of sardine poop," Quigley explained, "which I've discovered has the same properties as sardines' scales, so when we wear them, the material shimmers and reflects the indoor lighting and we disappear."

"HUCK BEAKHOPPER?" They jumped as a loud voice suddenly shouted from inside the kitchen. "HUCK BEAKHOPPER, WHERE ARE YOU?" They shrank back into the shadow of the truck as the flappy penguin with the row of pens around her neck who they'd seen earlier came flapping out the kitchen door.

"HUCK BEAKHOPPER?" she yelled again.

The door of the refrigerated truck's cab suddenly burst open. "I'm here!" And the driver appeared, straightening his overalls and flicking the sleep out of his eyes.

"Huck!" the flappy penguin said. "I just wanted to remind you of the running order for tonight." She flicked over a page on her clipboard. "The guests have begun arriving. We're serving them flocktails in the bar right now. In half an hour, you need to bring in the ice sculptures, just before they sit down for dinner. That way the sculptures won't melt. Then, once the guests are in their seats, Ms. Belle will do the big reveal."

Jackson's eyes widened. *The big reveal? Was that when they'd bring in the stolen fish?*

The flappy penguin glanced at her watch. "So, I'll call on you in thirty minutes. Make sure you're ready. Ms. Belle can't bear anyone being late. I've arranged for a group of waiters to help you carry in the sculptures. Come with me now and I'll introduce you." She led the driver off into the restaurant.

Jackson looked at the sardine suit again. *Could it work? Would it work?* Time was running out. They HAD to get inside. "Come on, Agent Q," Jackson said, pulling on the suit. "Let's do this!" He grimaced at the smell. "Next time, could you add deodorizers?"

But Quigley had already put his hood up. "Ready?" he said, his voice muffled behind the fabric. "Prepare to disappear, 00Zero."

They shuffled into the kitchen, their suits making a loud *shish-shish* sound as they moved. *Luckily*, Jackson thought, *the clanging and banging of the kitchen pots and pans probably drowns out the noise. Flippers crossed!* He blinked under the bright lights. The place was enormous— about four times the size of Jackson's kitchen at home, with at least a dozen chefs spread out along the workbenches, chopping, dicing, slicing, and stirring. Jackson tried to see what they were working on, but luckily none of the food looked like the missing fish.

Jackson froze as a chef suddenly turned to carry a tray of buns to a serving hatch on the other side of the kitchen. But the chef didn't notice him and Quigley. *Of course he didn't*, Jackson reminded himself, *because we're invisible.* He glanced at Quigley. *Huh?* Strangely, he could still see his buddy. Jackson wasn't sure why that was—surely, if they were both invisible, he shouldn't be able to see him. Jackson's heart started to beat a little faster. *Unless*... But there was no time to query this point with Quigley because just at that moment a waiter dashed into the kitchen.

"The boss is coming!" he hissed to the chefs. "She's doing an inspection. Stand up straight. Don't talk."

Jackson just had time to drag Quigley behind two dessert carts as a sudden jangling of heavy gold jewelry sounded down the corridor, a whiff of stinky perfume filled the air, and then Coldfinger swept into the room. No one moved. No one breathed. Even the pots seemed to stop bubbling as Coldfinger stalked around the workbenches, glaring at the chefs' work. "Too thick!" she snapped, pointing to some sliced sea greens. "Start over!"

"Too large!" she barked about a tray of krill buns. "Start over!"

"Too flowery!" she bawled over a tray of frosted tomatoes cut into tiny rose shapes. She flipped the tray onto the floor. "Start over!"

She carried on around the room, criticizing everything she saw, knocking over trays, upending mixing bowls, and yelling at her staff.

Jackson held his breath as she got closer and closer to their carts. *She won't be able to see us*, he told himself. *We're invisible. We've completely disappeared. She's looking at the strawberry sea mousse on the carts, not at you. No way has she seen you . . .*

Coldfinger let out a sudden shriek. She raised
one large, gold-covered flipper and pointed it
straight at Jackson and Quigley. "Intruders!"

"Uh—I don't think we're actually invisible,"
Jackson muttered to Quigley, his heart beginning to thump in his chest.

"Really?" His buddy cocked his head to one
side. "That's odd. Perhaps they don't have the
right lighting in here. Hey, let go!" Two burly
chefs had gotten ahold of them and were
yanking them out from behind the carts.

"What is that disgusting smell?" Coldfinger sniffed the whiff of fish poop escaping from their suits.

"We're not the only smelly things in here," Quigley said, covering his beak. "Your perfume is awful!"

"Trick or treat!" Jackson interrupted, breaking the secret-agent rule of dealing with dangerous situations by staying silent. Instead he said the first thing that popped into his head. "Happy EARLY Halloween! We're zombie sardines." He wiggled his sardine-stinky flippers at Coldfinger. "Smell our rotting fish skin. OOOO! Zombieeees," he added in what he hoped was a ghostly zombie-sardine sort of a voice.

"Enough!" Coldfinger hissed. "Get them out of here before I feed them to my sharks!"

"Sharks?" Quigley muttered. "Do you really have sharks?"

"Hey, let go!" Jackson tried to wriggle out of the chef's flippers as he dragged Jackson toward the kitchen door. Out of the corner of his eye, Jackson spotted something lying on the workbench. Something interesting . . . He just had time to grab it before the chef heaved him through the kitchen door and out, head-first into a giant snowdrift.

Seconds later, Quigley landed with a thump next to him.

"Well, I'm glad to be out of there," Quigley said. "I think I'm allergic to Coldfinger's perf—*Achoooo!*"

But Jackson didn't look up. He was too busy peering at the thing he'd grabbed.

"Look," he breathed. "A menu!"

"This is it," Jackson said, shaking off his hood so he could see better. "Evidence! If I could only turn the pages to look . . . *sheesh!* My flippers keep getting stuck to it."

"Want some help?" said a voice.

Jackson glanced up. "Lily!"

"Why are you wearing those weird sheets?" Lily leaned closer and grimaced. "You smell really bad."

"Sorry, but that information is classified," Quigley said, standing up and trying to dust the snow off his suit. But it didn't work. The snow was stuck fast.

"What are you doing here?" Jackson asked Lily.

She shrugged. "I wanted to see if your theory about the restaurant stealing the fish was right. And, well—" She looked at her feet. "I didn't want to stay at home. Dad's still not back. And Mom's been on the phone all evening trying to find out when he will be released. So I snuck out— Hey, is that a menu?" Lily peered at the booklet in Jackson's lap. "Can I see?" She crouched down next to him and unpeeled his sticky sardine flippers from the front cover. She angled the menu upward so she could read it in the light from the kitchen door. "Oh, no," she breathed. "Listen to this: Atlantic Koi Carp Kebabs. Jade Lobster Jell-O. Stink Squid Sorbet . . . They HAVE stolen the fish."

"I knew it!" Jackson gritted his beak. "And soon they'll have gobbled up the evidence." He stumbled to his feet, his snow-clad sardine suit feeling heavier than one of his dad's sea-cabbage cupcakes. "Come on, we've got to stop them. Let's do this!"

"Wait—what's that noise?" Quigley held up his flippers to silence Jackson and Lily. "Sounds like a whole bunch of snowmobiles arriving at the front of the restaurant."

"Maybe the FBI is doing a raid!" Lily's eyes sparkled with hope. "They told Mom they were putting all their best people on the case."

Jackson glanced at Quigley. If only Lily knew that THEY were the FBI's best people. The FBI didn't quite know it yet, but soon they would.

"I'm going to look." Lily set off across the parking lot, the two giant snow-covered sardines hopping after her. Around the side of the building they were blinded by camera flashes and headlights. A red carpet leading up to the front door of the restaurant had been laid out, and expensive snowmobiles were lined up at the end of it, dropping off their passengers.

"Oh, my word!" Lily gasped. "That's Justin Beaker."

"Who?" Quigley peered at the teenage penguin with a well-gelled crest who was posing on the red carpet.

"A pop penguin," Jackson muttered. He coughed and cleared his throat. "I only know because Finola likes him."

"There's Ice-P!" Lily gasped. "He's a rapper," she added for Quigley's benefit. "And oh, look, there's Pen-zella. I LOVE her blub."

"What's a blub?" Quigley scratched his crest.

"Seriously?" Lily's eyes widened. "A blub is an Ice-net posting where penguins write about their lives. Don't you follow any celebrity blubbers?"

"Look who else I see," Jackson interrupted.

Quigley groaned. "Hoff Rockface from school. What's he doing here?"

"I think that's his dad with him," Jackson said, craning his neck to check out the even larger version of Hoff Rockface who was climbing out of a shiny off-road snowmobile with sharp iceberg bumpers on the front. "I guess Coldfinger's invited rich businesspeople as well as celebrities to the opening of her restaurant."

The Rockfaces owned the Windy Tail Pier and the funfair, and secretly Jackson suspected Mr. Rockface wasn't entirely honest. Jackson didn't know many penguins who had won much in his amusement arcade slot machines.

Lily nudged Jackson. "Do you think those

penguins know they're going to eat my dad's fish?"

Jackson shrugged. "I don't think famous celebrity penguins like Justin Beaker would want to eat endangered species. They probably think they've just been invited to an expensive new restaurant serving unusual food. But I'm not so sure about Hoff Rockface and his dad. They're so mean, I bet they'd love to scarf rare fish!"

"That's terrible!" Lily cried. "We need to call the FBI right now. We've got to find a phone."

"But the FBI won't listen to us," Jackson said. "You saw what happened when we tried to tell them earlier. The FBI would need real proof before they would do anything."

"What about the menu?" Lily said. "That's proof!"

Quigley shook his head. "Not really.

Coldfinger could just say the names were meant as a joke."

"He's right," Jackson said. "Lots of restaurants give their food funny names. Like Brain Freezers. The Blue Whale Ice Whip isn't actually made of squashed blue whales."

Quigley nodded. "I used to think it was. But then I did some DNA analysis and discovered Blue Whale whips are just made of marshmallow."

Lily glanced at Jackson in disbelief. "Um—okay . . ." She puffed out her cheeks. "So, what exactly are we going to do about the fish? We can't just let those rich penguins eat them."

Jackson scratched his mangled crest. "Somehow, we're going to have to get back inside the restaurant."

They stood in silence for a moment, watching guests walking up the red carpet.

"Couldn't we just pretend to be famous?" Lily asked.

Jackson pointed to the flappy penguin with the pens around her neck. She was now standing at the front door with her two clipboards, checking off names. "I think there's a guest list," Jackson said.

The snow had started falling heavily again. Jackson tried to shake it off his sardine suit, but it stuck where it fell. "Think we might have to lose these now," he said, tugging at

his outfit. "It's so heavy with the snow stuck
to it."

"And you do look kind of weird," Lily said.
"Sort of sparkly, like the ice sculptures at my
Aunt Annie's wedding last year."

"Huh?" Jackson stopped tugging at the
suit. "Ice sculptures?" He glanced at Quigley,
looking at the way the snow had stuck to his
buddy's outfit. And how the lights from the
snowmobiles' headlights made it glisten like
ice. Lily was right—they did look a bit like ice

sculptures. Jackson felt the pulse of a plan slide through his body. Could their suits get them carried right into the heart of the Shark's Pit Restaurant? Jackson pushed his hood back up. "Quick!" he told Quigley. "Roll around in the snow and make sure your suit is completely covered. I think I've just thought of the BEST plan ever!"

"**A**re you sure this will work?" Lily whispered as they stood in the shadows next to the refrigerated truck.

"It's got to." Jackson peeped around the side of the truck sled. The driver and his helpers had just carried in two more of the ice sculptures, and the truck was nearly empty now. "Ready, Quigley?"

"Sure." His buddy nodded. "Just wanted to check—what's the backup?"

The backup! Jackson groaned. He'd broken the most basic FBI rule: ALWAYS have a backup plan. Jackson sighed. Uncle Bryn would never make that mistake. *Wait—of course! Uncle Bryn!* "The backup is my Uncle Bryn," he told Quigley. He glanced at Lily. "He—um—well, he knows some penguins who work for the FBI," he told her. No way could he blow Uncle Bryn's cover.

"Oh, yeah," Quigley said, winking at Jackson. "His Uncle Bryn works in the FBI gift shop."

Huh? Jackson did a double take at his buddy.

Lily smiled. "The FBI 'gift shop'?"

"Sure," Jackson said, not quite looking Lily in the eye. "But Uncle Bryn knows how to get in touch with real FBI secret agents."

"Yeah, because they're always popping in and out of his gift shop," Quigley explained, "buying spy sweaters and secret-agent stationary and, um, little boxes of FBI candy."

Lily looked like she was trying not to laugh. "Okay, so how do I get in touch with your uncle who works in the FBI *gift shop?*" She made little quotation marks in the air when she said *gift shop.*

Jackson considered this for a moment. He definitely didn't want to give her Uncle Bryn's top-secret cell number. Then he remembered something. "Inside my backpack, under my sardine suit, there's a transmitter. It belongs to Uncle Bryn."

Lily lifted up the back of Jackson's suit and began to rummage around in his backpack.

"It's in the top pocket," Jackson said. "Yep, that one. When you find it you'll see an emergency button on the side of the transmitter."

"That's the secret-agent locater button," Quigley added. "If you press it, the FBI will come and find us."

"So, if we're not back in"—Jackson glanced at his ice watch—"say, thirty minutes, press the button, okay?"

Lily held the transmitter up to the light. "Wow, the FBI 'gift shop' really looks after its staff. By the way, why have you got a bowling ball in your backpack?"

"Huh?" Jackson reached around and patted his backpack under his sardine suit. He felt something hard—the egg! He'd forgotten all about it. It had been so quiet in his backpack, probably snoozing (the egg slept a lot), that he'd forgotten it was still in there. He was just about to ask Lily to take his soon-to-be sibling out and look after it for him when the driver and his helpers suddenly reappeared through the restaurant doors. The friends shrank back into the shadows as the restaurant staff clambered up into the refrigerated truck, reappearing seconds later with two more ice sculptures on wooden boards.

"This one weighs more than Coldfinger's earrings," Jackson heard one of the waiters laughing.

"Watch it, buddy," the other one muttered. "If she hears you, she'll feed you to her sharks."

Jackson shuddered. Did she really have sharks inside the restaurant? *I guess we're about to find out*, he thought.

As soon as they'd gone, Jackson nudged Quigley. "Quick!" he whispered. "Let's do this!"

There were only a few ice sculptures left now. As Jackson hoisted himself up into the back, he spotted a pile of wooden boards propped up against the side. "Grab one of those," he whispered to Quigley.

"What sort of pose shall I do?" Quigley asked, stepping onto his board. "Teapot? Starfish? Diving seabird?"

Before Jackson could reply, they heard the footsteps of the returning driver and his helpers. Jackson just had time to take up his own position—a surfer pose, with both flippers held out to the sides—before the waiters climbed back up into the truck.

"Quick, guys," the driver called. "The guests are about to sit down in the restaurant. We've got to hurry."

Jackson hardly dared breathe as the waiters dragged his board toward the truck doors. Then, "One, two, heave!" and moments later he found himself being carried aloft, through the restaurant doors. Out of the corner of his eye he saw Lily in the shadows. She gave him a flippers-up as he passed, but Jackson could see the worried expression on her face.

Don't move, he told himself as he was carried along a gloomy hallway. *Don't blink. Don't breathe!* They passed through two sets of double doors and down another dark corridor into the belly of the building, until—

Oh, my gosh. Jackson gulped, trying not to blink in the light. *This is it. The Shark's Pit Restaurant.*

Jackson's eyeballs ping-ponged around
the enormous dining room. Giant ceiling-to-
floor glass tanks containing real, live great white
sharks the size of bus snowmobiles surrounded
the room. The sharks swam toothily past, their
giant tails slapping against the glass as though
they were trying to smash their way into the
restaurant so they could gobble up the guests
when they came in for dinner. *No way could
I eat with them licking their lips at me*, Jackson
thought. He noticed that the ice sculptures
had been laid out between the dinner tables.

They sparkled in the candlelight from the glittering chandeliers. *But where are the fish?* Jackson wondered. *If they're not in the kitchen and they're not in here, then—* Jackson gulped. Maybe he was wrong. Perhaps Coldfinger had

had nothing to do with the missing fish. If that was the case, then he'd need to come up with a pretty brilliant escape plan, pronto! Otherwise, Lily would call the FBI and he'd have a lot of explaining to do.

"Put it on there," said a familiar voice. It was the flappy penguin with the pens around her neck. She gestured to a plinth next to the largest table in the room. "Put that other one next to it," the flappy penguin added, pointing out a place for Quigley, too. She stood back and peered at them both. "Gee, I guess the ice sculptor was having an off day when she made these two."

Jackson felt his face burning. *Is she onto us?* He glanced at Quigley out of the corner of his eye and his heart missed a beat. *No way!* Quigley had gone for a running-penguin-on-one-leg pose. Jackson groaned inside. Admittedly, Quigley held the school record for the penguin who could stand on one leg the longest, thanks to his having figured out the mathematical equation for the angle at which to lean to ensure the best balance, but still . . . Was this the place to show off your one-leg standing skills? Jackson didn't think so. Mind you, his own surfer pose wasn't much better. His outstretched flippers were already beginning to feel like he was holding a snowmobile truck on each wing. He gritted his beak. *Do not move,* he told himself. *No matter how much your flippers hurt, you cannot move.*

Just then the restaurant doors opened and the dinner guests began to come in and sit down. Across the room he caught Hoff Rockface staring at him. *Uh-oh!* But seconds later, Hoff's attention was taken by a passing waiter carrying a basket of krill buns, and Jackson could breathe again.

"Ladies and gentle-penguins!" the flappy penguin shouted as the last guest took their seat. "Thank you so much for coming to the grand opening of the exclusive Shark's Pit Restaurant. Please put your flippers together to welcome your host for tonight's gala dinner, the owner of this exciting new restaurant, Ms. Chilla Belle!"

The guests burst into applause as Coldfinger shuffled out of the shadows, her blingy jewelry sparkling under the lights and her foul, sickly-sweet perfume wafting around the room. Jackson held his breath as she came and stood right next to him. "Good evening, friends," she barked. Her voice was rough and deep, like she'd been gargling with gravel. Jackson felt a hot wave of fear pass through his sardine suit. He hoped it wouldn't melt the snow. "Tonight you are in for the treat of a lifetime,"

Coldfinger growled. "You will experience food that no other penguins have ever tried before!"

As she spoke, Jackson felt a sudden thump in his backpack. *Oh, no! Coldfinger's voice must have woken the egg. Please go back to sleep,* he willed his soon-to-be sibling.

"These spectacular dishes will be prepared by the most exceptional chefs from around the world." Coldfinger snapped her flippers and six penguins wearing aprons and tall white hats marched into the room, bowing to the guests. "They will cook the most unusual delicacies for your delight." Jackson glanced briefly at Quigley. The "most unusual delicacies"? She had to be talking about the stolen fish. But if she was, where were they?

"In my restaurant, we serve exceptional food for exceptional penguins!" Coldfinger grinned at her guests, who roared their approval, clapping and whooping.

The egg did a complete flip at the noise, nearly unbalancing Jackson. *STOP MOVING!* he wished he could yell, *OR YOU'LL BLOW MY COVER!* He made a mental note NEVER to bring a junior agent on a mission again.

Coldfinger held up her flippers for silence. "Everything will be prepared fresh at your table," she rasped as more chefs marched in, pushing large hot plates on wheels. "And now, to reveal the ingredients." She clapped her flippers three times and a large circle in the middle of the floor began to slide back.

The guests craned their necks to see what was happening. So did Jackson. He blinked in wonder as a wide, water-filled glass cylinder at least ten feet in diameter began to rise up and out of the floor. And inside—Jackson's eyes boggled, and he felt his feathers stiffen and his beak fall open—were the missing fish!

They were all there. The koi. The lobster. The crabs and the seahorse. And others, too. Iridescent jellyfish. Rainbow-colored rays. And the stink-ink squid with the neon-yellow legs that was glaring out miserably from the bottom of the tank.

"Take your pick!" Coldfinger cried, pointing to the tank. "Choose your favorite unusual ingredients from my tank, and my chefs will fish them out and create the most exclusive finger foods you've ever—"

But before she could finish her sentence, there was an enormous *Achoooo!* and Quigley fell off his plinth.

17

The whole room froze.

"It's her perfume," Quigley explained. "I'm allergic!"

"Don't worry, Agent Q," Jackson said, hopping off his plinth. "We've seen enough." He flipped off his hood and pointed at Coldfinger. "I'm Secret Agent 00Zero. On behalf of the FBI, I'm arresting you for theft of endangered species."

The guests gasped. The chefs began to back out of the room. But Coldfinger wasn't beaten. She started to erupt. First her flippers waggled, then her belly shook, and finally her beak snapped open, frothy spit spluttering out when she said, "HOW DARE YOU!"

"We've got the evidence," Quigley said, pulling out his Blink Cam Goggles. "Or we soon will have. Smile for the camera!" He began taking pictures of Coldfinger and the guests and the stolen fish.

"You're going down," Jackson told Coldfinger. "For a long time."

"LIES! All lies!" Coldfinger spun around to the guests, her furious face softening a fraction. "These fish aren't stolen. These horrible hatchlings are intruders. Sneaky paparazzi trying to get pictures of you, my lovely, famous friends, so they can sell them to celebrity gossip magazines."

The dinner guests began to boo and shout at Jackson and Quigley.

"Hey!" Jackson cried as a krill bun bounced off his head, followed by several more.

"I know them," Hoff Rockface shouted, firing more buns at them. "They're the loser patrol from school."

"SECURITY!" Coldfinger bellowed. "Get them out of here!"

"Code Red, Agent Q," Jackson shouted as four muscle penguins appeared from the shadows. "Run!"

They raced across the room, guests screaming, krill buns flying, and Coldfinger's security guards chasing after them.

"Through here!" Jackson headed down a corridor full of stacked dining chairs. "Hey, take a seat," he shouted to the guards behind him as he pulled a few piles down, blocking their path. It worked—for about a heartbeat. But the security penguins just charged over the chairs, cursing and yelling, and were immediately back on their tails.

"It's a dead end," Quigley puffed out as they reached the end of the corridor. "We'll have to go up the stairs."

Jackson hesitated. They needed to get OUT, not go up!

"Don't worry," Quigley said, already halfway up the first flight. "If we end up on the roof, I'm wearing parachute underwear—two pairs."

Jackson grimaced. He did NOT want to borrow Quigley's underwear. "I guess there might be a fire escape." He crossed his flippers and dived after Quigley.

"GET THEM!" The biggest security penguin was right behind them now. He lunged. "Gotcha!" He grabbed Jackson's sardine suit.

"No way!" Jackson put his head down and powered forward. There was a loud *r-i-p-p*-ing sound and Jackson slipped from the guard's clutches, leaving him holding half a sticky sardine suit.

"Grrrr!" The guard tried to flick it off his flippers, but it was stuck fast. The other guards pushed past him.

"I don't think so," Quigley muttered, fiddling with his watch's strap. He shook his wrist and a jet of black oil splattered onto the steps below him. "Octopus ink—super-slidey!" He grinned at Jackson as the guards began to slip. And slide and—

"Arghhh!" The guard in front lost his footing altogether and fell backward, crashing into the three guards behind him like an enormous black-and-white bowling ball.

"Strike!" Jackson shouted. "Ten-pin take-down! Great work, Agent Q."

They hopped up the last few steps and along the landing.

"Through here?" Jackson pulled open the first door they came to and they slipped inside. "I can't see much," Jackson whispered, his eyes blinking in the strange blue light. "Whoa—look at the glass floor. I think we're above the shark tanks."

Quigley peered down through his toes at the large, dark shapes swimming underneath.

"Urgh," Jackson groaned. "Check this out." He pointed to a bucket of disgusting chum next to a hatch in the middle of the floor. "I guess this is where they feed them. We've got to get out of here."

"Too late," said a cold voice across the room, and Coldfinger stepped out of the shadows. In her flippers was a long, sharp pole. The fish-grabber claw!

"But how did you get in here?" Jackson said.

Coldfinger snorted. "First rule in the bad-guy handbook: always have a back door." She gestured behind her. As she spoke, the other door burst open and the disheveled muscle penguins barged in. "Sorry, boss, we nearly had them."

"Silence!" Coldfinger extended the grabber claw to poke the front guard in the chest. "I'll deal with you later."

"N-n-not the shark tank," he gasped.

"We'll see," she hissed. Then she moved

the claw to point at Jackson and Quigley. "So you worked it out, did you? I should have known. You smelled like trouble the first time I saw you."

"WE smelled like trouble?" Quigley pushed the Blink Cam Goggles onto the top of his head. "You should smell yourself sometime— *poooo-eeeee!*" He held his beak with his flipper. "That perfume is worse than seal pee. Mind you, it's not really your fault. Older penguins lose their smell receptors, you see. They decrease with age. That's why grandma penguins always put on too much perfume—"

"Quigley," Jackson whispered, "I don't think this is helping."

Coldfinger's face had ballooned with fury.

"Not that you look like a grandma penguin," Quigley added. "Well, apart from the earrings. My grandma has the exact same pair."

"Quiet!" Coldfinger poked Quigley's belly

with the grabber claw. "Give me that camera!"

"What? These?" Quigley reached for his Blink Cam Goggles. "No way. It took me six months to make them."

Jackson stepped in front of his buddy. "And the goggles are FBI evidence now. As soon as they get here, we'll be handing the pictures to them."

Coldfinger rolled her eyes. "'As soon as they get here'? Oh, yes, right—because the FBI is always on speed dial for pesky little hatchlings." She shook her head. "Now give me those goggles or I'll feed you to my sharks."

Jackson grabbed the glasses off Quigley's head and jumped forward, snapping open the shark-feeding hatch with his toes. "By the time you've fished them out of here," he said, dangling them above the hole, "the FBI will have arrived to arrest you." *Flippers crossed the sharks don't eat them first!*

Coldfinger smiled a strange, cruel smile, which made her eyes almost disappear into the creases of her face. "Before you do anything stupid," she said quietly, "I think I might have something you'd like to trade for. Small hatchlings love to trade, don't they?"

Jackson scowled at her. Did Coldfinger really think he was going to swap the Blink Cam Goggles, which had proof of Coldfinger's crimes that they could show to the FBI, for a few rare flipper-ball collector cards? She obviously didn't know who she was dealing with.

"Look over there," Coldfinger said, gesturing to one of her security guards. "I think you might have dropped something on the stairs."

Jackson followed her gaze and his heart stopped. "Nooooo!"

The guard was holding what looked like—

"The egg," he whispered. "But that's impossible." Jackson reached up to feel for his backpack. But it was gone. He gritted his beak. The guard must have ripped it off when he'd torn Jackson's sardine suit.

Coldfinger let out a long, low cackle that made her earrings jangle. "Whoever hired you as an egg-sitter is going to be so disappointed. I'm not sure you'll get hired again. Now give me those goggles or I'll feed you AND your little eggy friend to the sharks."

Jackson tried to shout, *That's not fair!* But the words got stuck in his throat. He looked at Quigley. His buddy shrugged. Coldfinger had them.

Or did she?

Jackson took a deep breath. Secret agents never gave up. And neither did big brothers. He puffed up his feathers. His mangled crest stood tall, spiky, and alert. There was a strange, pulsating anger growing in his belly, getting larger by the second. NO ONE, no matter how

evil and scary, or however large their earrings, could threaten his soon-to-be sibling and get away with it. The bubble of fury in his belly suddenly shot up Jackson's throat and burst out of his beak in a "GARGGGGGGHHHH!" Then he tossed the goggles into the shark tank and shouted, "CODE ICE STORM!" to Quigley. *Code Ice Storm* meant *attack*, but his buddy was already on it. Quigley had his backpack open and a whole swarm of frost-wasp bots was escaping.

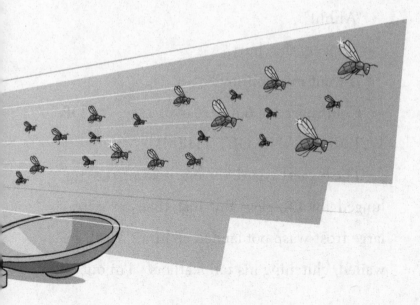

"I borrowed them from Sunny's workshop!" Quigley explained to Jackson. "I added the control box; awesome, right? See, it works by—"

"Great!" Jackson interrupted. "But maybe save the explanation for later."

"Sure thing." Quigley flicked a switch and—

"Ow!" squealed one of the muscle penguins as a bot stung him.

"Stop!"

"No!" another guard yelled.

"Not frost wasps! I hate frost wasps!"

"Ahhh!"

"Eeeeee, that hurt."

"I want my mommy!"

Coldfinger let out a roar of rage. "STOP WHINING AND GET THEM!"

The biggest guard, the one holding the egg, lunged for Quigley. But just then an extra-large frost-wasp bot landed on him. "Yow!" he wailed, clutching his tail feathers. "I'm out of here!" He dropped the egg and shuffled out of the room, quickly followed by the other guards and the swarm of bots.

Jackson scooped up his soon-to-be sibling. But Coldfinger wasn't beaten. She dived toward him, spinning the grabber claw wildly above her head. "Hey, barf-beak, how do you like your eggs? How about scrambled!"

Jackson backed away, shielding the egg. Then his legs bumped into something that smelled foul. He glanced down. *Of course!* He signaled to Quigley. "Catch!" And he bowled his soon-to-be sibling across the floor to his buddy. Then he grabbed the bucket of shark chum and shouted, "Hey, Coldfinger! You look hungry. Have some snacks."

For a second she didn't seem to know what had hit her. Then the icky gloop started trickling down her face. "My jewels," she shrieked, dropping the grabber claw and clutching her bling.

"Ms. Belle?" The flappy penguin with the pens around her neck poked her head around the door. "Oh my word!" she gasped when she saw Coldfinger. "What on earth—"

"Help me!" Coldfinger wailed.

"Ooo, I'd love to," the flappy penguin said. "But the FBI has just arrived. And they want to see you."

"What? No!" Coldfinger's eyes widened. "Order my heli-hopper. I'm leaving!" She shuffled past Jackson.

"Not so fast!" Jackson scooped up the grabber claw, and before Coldfinger could reach the door he'd hooked her by the ankles. She hit the floor with a loud jangly *doof!*

"Let me go!" Coldfinger growled, thrashing about like a beached whale.

"I don't think so," said a familiar voice. Jackson's Uncle Bryn stood in the doorway with three other FBI agents, a beaming Lily behind him. She gave them a flippers-up.

Uncle Bryn pushed his dark glasses down a fraction and winked at his nephew. "Good work there, young agents," he said. "Ms. Chilla Belle, I'm Agent Rockflopper of the FBI. We've seen everything downstairs. You are under arrest for theft of rare species."

"How dare you!" Coldfinger spluttered.

"Take her away, fellas," Uncle Bryn told his colleagues.

"What? No!" Coldfinger yelled. "Get those flipper-cuffs off me!" Coldfinger tried to kick Uncle Bryn as she was led away. "After my lawyers have finished with you, you'll be working in a gift shop."

"He already does." Lily grinned at Jackson and Quigley.

"Well, you guys certainly netted a good catch there," Uncle Bryn said after Coldfinger had gone.

"I agree." The FBI boss penguin shuffled in. "Good work, hatchlings!"

Jackson blushed. This time he didn't mind being called a hatchling.

"We've had our eye on Chilla Belle for years," she added. "But we've never had the evidence to arrest her for anything until now."

"Oh, you'll find lots of evidence on my Blink

Cam Goggles," Quigley said, "only they're at the bottom of this shark tank."

"But we can fish the goggles out for you with this." Jackson waggled the grabber claw. "And we can show you how she stole the fish, too. See, we discovered that there are these drainage tunnels that connect to the aquarium next door."

Uncle Bryn's boss cracked a smile. "We may need to think about starting a junior agent division at the FBI, Agent Rockflopper," she told Uncle Bryn. "I think these two might make good recruits."

Jackson and Quigley looked at each other. *Have we done it? Have we actually gotten ourselves hired by the FBI?* Jackson wondered.

But just then there was a cough from the doorway. "Excuse me, but it's WAY past their bedtime. Jackson! Quigley! I think you've got some explaining to do."

Jackson gulped.

Quigley gasped.

Even Uncle Bryn and his boss looked scared.

"Hi, Mom," Jackson squeaked. "I can explain everything."

Lily's dad sure looked happy when he arrived to fetch his fish," Jackson said.

His mom nodded but didn't say anything as she drove them out of the restaurant parking lot, heading for home.

"Oh, yeah," Quigley said. "His fish are safe, the real thief is behind bars, and he's got his job back."

"Mmm," Jackson's mom said, glancing at them both in her rearview mirror.

"Wish we could have stayed and helped him and Lily return the fish to the aquarium," Jackson added.

His mom frowned at him in her mirror, but she didn't say anything.

Jackson glanced at Quigley. So far his mom hadn't actually gone Great White on them, but they both knew it was bound to happen any moment. The wait before getting their heads chewed off was always worse than the actual head chewing itself.

Jackson sighed. He wanted to have it over and done with. "Hey, did you hear that Uncle Bryn said most of the guests at the restaurant didn't even know the fish on the menu were protected species?"

"I bet Hoff Rockface and his dad did," Quigley said. "They looked pretty smug as they were leaving."

"Hmm," Jackson's mom said. But she still didn't say anything.

Jackson looked at his buddy again. This was agony—like the calm before the snowstorm!

"At least Sunny isn't in trouble," Jackson went on. "Uncle Bryn says he had no idea what Coldfinger was planning to do with the fish grabber."

"Such a relief," Quigley said. "If he'd gone to jail, he wouldn't have been able to fix my sled."

"Oh, yeah, that would have been terrible." Jackson smiled. Secretly he hoped Sunny would never get around to mending it. He definitely didn't want another test drive, not after Sunny had gotten his flippers on it.

Quigley nudged him. "Lily said to give you this."

Jackson took the FBI transmitter his buddy was holding and quickly shoved it in his backpack before his mom saw it. *Must remember to give that back to Uncle Bryn sometime,* he thought. Although it had come in handy. Lily had said the FBI arrived less than three minutes after she'd pressed the button.

Jackson looked at his mom again in her mirror. *Still no head chewing?* Then a hopeful thought popped into his head. Maybe she wasn't going to go Great White after all. Maybe she was actually proud of them. Maybe she wouldn't mind them joining the FBI. Jackson took a deep breath. "So, the FBI said we could maybe join them as junior agents," he said as though it was a perfectly normal occupation for young penguins. *Please think this is a good idea,* he thought, crossing his flippers.

"HA! Great joke, Jackson," his mom suddenly exploded. "As if I'd let you put yourselves in danger like that. Not to mention the egg!" She glanced across at Jackson's soon-to-be sibling, who was sitting in a car seat next to her. "What were you boys thinking, taking the egg with you?" Her words shot out like hailstones. "ANYTHING could have happened! What if the egg had hatched?"

Jackson looked at his feet. "Sorry, Mom."

"Yeah, sorry, Mrs. Rockflopper," Quigley said. He glanced at Jackson and mouthed, *Great White!*

"Well, you're both going to have plenty of time to think about your behavior," Jackson's mom snapped. And the atmosphere in the snowmobile suddenly plummeted to sub-zero. Jackson looked at Quigley. This was it. She was moving in for the kill.

"I've spoken to your parents, too, Quigley," she said. "And we all agreed upon your punishment." She paused for several frozen seconds and Jackson and Quigley held their breath. Then—"DECK SCRUBBING!" she bellowed.

"What? NOOOO!" Jackson couldn't believe his ears. Deck scrubbing meant cleaning up gull poop. Rookeryville was covered in the stuff.

"Oh, and I thought it would be a really nice gesture if you were to scrub ALL the decks in the neighborhood. Because you know, a really strange thing happened earlier." Jackson's mom pulled up outside their house and turned to face them, her eyes glinting and a toothy great-white smile washing over her face. "See, ALL the neighbors paid me a visit tonight. For some reason, they thought I was hosting a party. Can you believe it?"

Jackson glanced at Quigley and swallowed hard.

"There were dozens of them," she went on. "Such a coincidence, huh? Well, their visit gave me the idea for your punishment. I'm calling it Operation Good Neighbor. I'll wake you both at 5 A.M. tomorrow so you get an early start. You can begin with old Mrs. Hoppy-Floppy's deck at the end of the street."

"But, Mom," Jackson wailed. "Mrs. Hoppy-Floppy FEEDS the gulls. Her deck is, like, Poop City!"

"Oh, and Jackson"—his mom's shark eyes bored into his—"just for the record, I won the trackers' cup three years in a row when I was in Flipper Scouts." She winked at him. "So I will *always* find you, snow or no snow! Now, off to bed, both of you." Mom picked up the egg, slipped out of the snowmobile, and stalked up the path.

As they followed her to the house, their backs droopy and their beaks down, Jackson felt a sudden vibration in his backpack. It was Uncle Bryn's transmitter. Jackson grabbed Quigley and they hung back, listening to the radio.

"CALLING ALL AGENTS, CALLING ALL AGENTS," said a tiny, tinny voice from inside the bag. "WE HAVE REPORTS OF AN ALARM GOING OFF AT THE BEST CREST BANK. ALL AGENTS RESPOND."

"A bank robbery?" Jackson whispered.

"Awesome!" Quigley gave his buddy a flippers-up.

"As soon as Mom's asleep, we'll go check it out, right?"

"Sure thing, Agent 00Zero," Quigley whispered. "Just give me two minutes to fast-charge the frost-wasp bots, because you never know when they'll come in handy."

Jackson hopped up the last few steps and into the house with a giant grin on his face. He could feel his adventure detector starting to sound—a real-life bank robbery? *Yes, please!* "We're going to show the FBI that they need us," he whispered to Quigley. "And this time Mom is not going to stop us. Come on, LET'S DO THIS!"

Their next mission had begun.

ACKNOWLEDGMENTS

Just as Jackson and Quigley work together to solve crimes, so it takes a team to make a book about their adventures.

I'd like to thank my fantastic editor, Holly West, for her boundless enthusiasm, her expert direction, and her keen eye for detail. And also thanks to the rest of the team at Feiwel and Friends; I feel so lucky to be part of your family.

I'm grateful too for the work of talented artist Marek Jagucki, who brings Rookeryville to life with his amazing pictures.

I couldn't write without the support of my much-loved family, especially my husband, James, and my children, Alice and Archie, who have had to put up with my penguin obsession. Thanks, Alice, for your unwavering rock-solid belief in me. And thanks, Archie, for proofreading the first draft and for nagging me to get on with book 2 because you enjoyed the first story so much!

And finally, I'd like to thank my awesome agent, Gemma Cooper, who loved Jackson and Quigley's penguin world from the start. Thanks for your patience, encouragement, and support, Gemma. You're one special penguin.

GOFISH

QUESTIONS FOR THE AUTHOR

SAM HAY

Jackson and Quigley have very clear plans for their future. What did *you* want to be when you grew up?
I always wanted to be a writer. From as early as I can remember, I made up stories in my head. My bike was actually a horse (in my imagination), and together we'd ride off on adventures around the neighborhood! I kept loads of little notebooks crammed with my stories. Then when I was a teenager, one of my teachers suggested that a more short-term, practical job ambition might be to become a journalist first. It was good advice. Training as a journalist was the perfect way to sharpen my story-writing skills. I learned to write rapidly and succinctly.

What was your first job, and what was your "worst" job?
My first job was also my worst job. I was nine years old, and I got a job delivering free newspapers, which I did on my roller skates, until one day I whizzed too fast down someone's driveway and crashed into a pair of giant metal gates! Ouch!

Where did the initial idea for *Spy Penguins* come from?
I'm not sure. Penguins are one of my favorite animals, and I love spy stories! A couple of years ago, I visited a sea-life

sanctuary with my family, and I was fascinated by the complex community the penguins lived in—their friendships and relationships. And of course, they look a bit like James Bond with their natural dinner jackets!

Who is your favorite fictional spy?

Such a hard question because I have so many favorites! If I had to choose, I'd say Richard Hannay from the book *The Thirty-Nine Steps* by John Buchan and George Smiley from the John le Carré spy novels. They're both very different characters. Richard Hannay is brave and adventurous—quite like Jackson in *Spy Penguins*—while George Smiley is much more reflective, quiet, and mild-mannered, using his intelligence to solve cases. I also must mention Q, the genius gadget-maker from the James Bond novels. He was always my favorite character and an inspiration for Quigley in *Spy Penguins*!

If you were a spy, what would your code name be?

00-Pencils! I have a desk full of pencils—all of them very sharp! And if I was a spy, I'd write down all my adventures in tiny secret notebooks.

What is your favorite word?

My favorite words change all the time. I recently treated myself to an enormous new dictionary. It's so big I can barely lift it! It's very useful when I play scrabble. I can pull out lots of obscure words that fit into all the difficult spaces on the board. But my favorite words are often Scottish words. I grew up in Scotland, so I use a lot of the words we'd say at home. My favorite ones are *boorach* (a mess), *stooshie* (an argument) and *blether* (to talk). My kids aren't Scottish, so it's funny to hear them use the same words when they're talking to their friends.

What book is on your nightstand now?
As well as spy stories, I love detective fiction and I always have an Agatha Christie book on my nightstand. I've read them all, and I can usually remember the plots, but they're quite comforting and very entertaining.

What is the best advice you've ever received about writing?
The best bit of advice came from one of my lecturers at journalism college, a wise and lovely man named Bill Allsopp. He said, "You can have a bigger impact if you use fewer words." Basically, he meant that if you pad your writing with too much description and lots of waffle, you lose impact.

Where do you write your books?
I write at a very messy desk. It's covered in paper, pencils, and strange and interesting stuff that inspires me, such as a four-foot-tall plastic anatomical skeleton, a cute cuddly penguin toy my son gave me, and an antique barometer that never predicts the weather correctly. (Maybe it's predicting the weather in another world, somewhere much more exciting!)

What would your readers be most surprised to learn about you?
Two things! When I was a kid, one of my favorite places to hang out was a giant, Victorian graveyard, standing high above the Scottish city of Glasgow. It's called the Necropolis, and my granny used to take me and my brother there. It always seemed so atmospheric and full of stories!

I'm also *extremely* competitive when I play board games. I love to win! My kids are the same. When they play together, they have to pretend there is a third person playing, an imaginary opponent, so they can make that person lose!

I also *love* candy. Pear drops are my favorite. (Oops, that's three things. Sorry.)

When Uncle Bryn is suspected of being a master thief, it's up to **JACKSON** and **QUIGLEY** to solve the case!

SPY PENGUINS

THE SPY WHO LOVED ICE CREAM

SAM HAY

Illustrated by MAREK JAGUCKI

Keep reading for an excerpt.

Jackson lunged toward Hoff. But every time he moved, the skates scrubbed him backward.

Hoff and his friends exploded with laughter.

"Quigley!" Jackson hissed. "Do something!"

"Don't worry," Quigley said, pulling out a remote control. "I'll flick the switch to turbo mode!"

"What? *Argh!*" Rocket blasters shot out of the back of Jackson's skates and thrust him forward.

Hoff had stopped laughing. His eyes widened as Jackson, his hat spinning and his feet flying, came thundering toward him.

"Ahhhh!" Jackson yelled, even though he was breaking the basic rule of secret-agent survival: NEVER scream like you're scared!

But seeing as Jackson WAS scared, because he was heading straight for Mrs. Hoppy-Floppy's wooden fence, which was between him and Hoff, with no way of stopping, he couldn't help it. "Arghh!" he screamed louder. *Got to jump it!* Jackson told himself. *Got to jump the fence!*

But instead of jumping it, he *THWUMPED* it. BAM!

Jackson opened his eyes and gave his feathers a shake. *Nope. No bones broken.* And considering he'd just blasted halfway through a wooden fence at turbo speed, that was a pretty good outcome.

"Selfie!" Hoff's horrible face suddenly appeared next to his. "Smile for the camera!"

"What? No! Stop!"

But Hoff had already taken the photo. "Nice one, Jackson. You're a loser legend. Come on," he called to his friends. "I can't wait to post this on the school blub."

Jackson gritted his beak. The school had a

new Ice-net blub page where students could share news and events. Jackson groaned. He did NOT want to be today's headline story. He tried to scramble to his feet, then tripped over his skates and landed back in the broken fence. He could hear Hoff and his friends laughing their feathers off as they shuffled away.

"Oh, wow!" Quigley said, peering down at Jackson's head. "That crash-helmet inner lining I installed on the Poop Protector Hat really worked. See? There's not a mark on your head. Well, apart from two bent spoons. But I can fix them."

"Great!" Jackson tugged off the hat and skates and hauled himself up. "Shame you didn't install a Hoff-zapping device in it, too!" He looked at the broken fence, then over at the poopy deck, where even more gulls had arrived. "Guess we're not going to make Uncle Bryn's birthday party."

"Hello? Is everything okay?" They turned to find Mrs. Hoppy-Floppy standing behind them.

"Oh, um—hi." Jackson felt his face go shrimp pink. "I'm—err, so sorry about your fence. You see, we were trying out some new deck-scrubbing equipment—"

"My new inventions!" Quigley interrupted. "To get the job done faster."

"But they went a bit wrong and—"

"It's all right," Mrs. Hoppy-Floppy said. "But I think that's enough deck scrubbing for today. In fact, I think that's enough for the rest of the vacation."

"But what about your fence?" Jackson began. "We can fix it—"

"No!" Mrs. Hoppy-Floppy interrupted. "Absolutely not!" She steadied herself against the remaining fence post. "It's very kind of you to want to help, but my son will fix the fence. Why don't you boys go home now?"

Jackson couldn't believe his ears. "Are you sure?"

Mrs. Hoppy-Floppy nodded.

"And you won't tell his mom?" Quigley added.

"I'll tell her you were very helpful," Mrs. Hoppy-Floppy said. "So helpful that you never need come help again!"

"That was strange," Quigley whispered as they shuffled away. "It was almost like Mrs. Hoppy-Floppy didn't want our help."

"At least we won't miss the party," Jackson said, picking up his ice cycle from the grassy bank where they'd parked them. "Come on! Let's do this!"

The boys ducked their heads as they cycled past Jackson's house, just in case his dad was looking.

"Hey, was that a heli-hopper pad on the roof of your house?" Quigley said.

"Yeah, Dad just finished it." Jackson's dad loved to build new rooms onto their house. Last week, he'd added a smoothie-juicing room next to the kitchen, and before that he'd built a pottery-making den under the stairs. But the heli-hopper pad was Jackson's favorite; all secret agents needed to know how to fly a heli-hopper. "We haven't actually gotten a heli-hopper yet," Jackson explained. "But—"

"I could build you one!" Quigley interrupted. "Sunny could help me."

Jackson wobbled on his ice cycle. "N-n-no, it's okay, but thanks." Quigley's big cousin

Sunny was an even more dangerous inventor than Quigley. "So what are you going to order at Brain Freezers?" Jackson asked, changing the subject. "A triple-choc seaweed shake, maybe?"

They spotted Uncle Bryn as they pulled up outside the café.

"Cool! He bagged the window booth," Quigley said, chaining his ice cycle to a lamp-post. The window booth was their favorite seat at Brain Freezers. Mission Control, as they called it, was where Jackson and Quigley liked to plan their adventures.

"I don't see his boss, though," Jackson said. "Maybe she's coming later. Hey, Uncle Bryn," he called as they walked into the café. "Happy birthday!"

But his uncle didn't look up. Neither did his two colleagues. They just sat there staring straight ahead, spooning weird-looking ice cream into their beaks.

"Happy birthday, Uncle Bryn!" Jackson tapped him on the back. Still no response. Jackson glanced at Quigley, who shrugged. "Guys?" Jackson looked across the table at Uncle Bryn's work friends. But they just kept eating their ice cream—a strange-looking sort that Jackson had never seen before. It had yellow and green stripes, and—Jackson blinked—it glowed! "What flavor is that?" Jackson asked them.

But no one replied. No one moved. They just kept eating and staring.

"Maybe they're playing a party game?" Quigley whispered. "Like ice statues."

But Jackson didn't think so. His beak tingled. His danger detectors were going off again. There was something odd happening here. He just knew it.

"I like your new cap, Mr. Rockflopper," Quigley said to Jackson's uncle Bryn. "Did you get it for your birthday? Oh, wait, I see you've all got one." He nudged Jackson. "Hey, maybe they're giving caps away here today. I'll ask Victor." Quigley looked around the diner. "I don't see Victor, do you?"

Victor was the manager of Brain Freezers. He always liked to greet the customers himself.

"I don't see anyone I recognize," Jackson muttered. He stared at the two people serving behind the counter. They were both wearing the same sort of cap as Uncle Bryn and his colleagues, blue with a letter *F* embroidered on the front. "They must have hired new staff."

Uncle Bryn laid down his spoon and stood up. His two colleagues did the same. They pushed past the boys, heading for the door.

"Wait—Uncle Bryn," Jackson called. "Where are you going?"

But his uncle didn't reply. He kept walking, zombie-style, out the door.

Jackson and Quigley followed the agents out onto the sidewalk.

"Uncle Bryn! What's going on?" Jackson had a funny feeling in his tummy now—a sort of knot. Uncle Bryn NEVER ignored him. "Uncle Bryn? What's wrong? Why can't you speak?"

But Jackson's voice was drowned out by the rumble of an engine. An ice cream truck sled pulled up. The back doors clunked open and Uncle Bryn and his friends clambered in.

"Hey!" Jackson called. "Where are you going?"

But the truck sled had already zoomed off.